MEET THE FORTUNES

Fortune of the Month: Chloe Fortune Elliott

Age: 26

Vital statistics: Five foot two, eyes of blue and a heart as big as Texas.

Claim to Fame: None—until she discovers Jerome Fortune is her biological father.

Romantic prospects: Questionable. She has loved and lost. Once you've "fallen off the horse," it can be hard to pick yourself up again.

"I've been working as a counselor at Peter's Place ranch for just a few weeks now, and it's just as challenging—and rewarding—as I thought it would be. One challenge I *didn't* expect was Chance Howell. Graham Fortune's new ranch hand makes me feel, well...he makes me *feel*. I thought my heart died along with my husband when Donnie got killed in Afghanistan.

I suppose any red-blooded female would respond to a cowboy as sexy as Chance. But he's a former soldier himself, and he's made it clear he doesn't "do" permanent. And I'm still trying to wrap my mind around the fact that I'm a Fortune. There are a million reasons why we shouldn't get involved. So why do they go flying out the window the minute he sidles up beside me?"

THE FORTUNES OF TEXAS:
The Secret Fortunes—
A new generation of heroes and heartbreakers!

Dear Reader,

When I was growing up, my entire family, not counting me, consisted of four people: a pair of parents called Mama and Daddy and a pair of younger brothers (I asked my parents for pet dogs, but they couldn't afford them, so this was my consolation prize) called pains-in-the-neck. It wasn't until several years later that I found out they had names, Michael and Mark. Despite what I initially felt was a less than successful foray into siblinghood, I always wanted a large family, the kind that made finding parking places near the house around holiday time a tricky event. Unfortunately, things didn't quite work out. Consequently, I went from not having any uncles or aunts (and thus no cousins) to not having any nieces or nephews because neither brother got married. I did succeed in finding someone to love and we had two kids together, but that's a story for another time.

To make up for this lack of relatives in my life, I write about families with relatives. In the case of the Fortunes, theirs is a family saga on steroids. With a prolific patriarch as their father, the children of Gerald Robinson, finally revealed to be Jerome Fortune, cannot turn around in a full circle without finding another one of their father's offspring. What you have before you is the story of one such offspring: army widow Chloe Elliott, who only recently discovered that she has the same DNA as the very famous Fortune family. But DNA alone isn't enough when it comes to being accepted, at least not by the entire family. Come read and find out how she finally becomes a genuine part of the family while also finding the love of her life—again.

Thank you for taking the time to read one of my books, and from the bottom of my heart, I wish you someone to love who loves you back.

Love,

Marie Ferrarella

Fortune's Second-Chance Cowboy

Marie Ferrarella

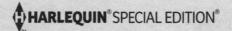
HARLEQUIN® SPECIAL EDITION®

Special thanks and acknowledgment
are given to Marie Ferrarella for her contribution
to the Fortunes of Texas: The Secret Fortunes continuity.

Recycling programs
for this product may
not exist in your area.

ISBN-13: 978-0-373-62332-7

Fortune's Second-Chance Cowboy

Copyright © 2017 by Harlequin Books S.A.

HARLEQUIN®
www.Harlequin.com

Printed in U.S.A.

USA TODAY bestselling and RITA® Award–winning author **Marie Ferrarella** has written more than two hundred and fifty books for Harlequin, some under the name Marie Nicole. Her romances are beloved by fans worldwide. Visit her website, marieferrarella.com.

Visit the Author Profile page at Harlequin.com for more titles.

To
Tiffany Khauo,
who is about to have her own population explosion.
Tiffany, this one's for you.

Prologue

"Hello, Chloe, are you still there?"

Chloe Elliott's hand tightened around her landline's receiver as she heard the caller's deep male voice asking her the same question again.

Was she still there?

Part of Chloe felt like answering the question by simply hanging up. She'd had enough disappointments in her twenty-six years to last a lifetime, why would she set herself up for yet another one?

But there was this other part of Chloe, the part that *needed* to believe that good things could happen, that they still *did* happen. That was the part that had been instrumental in making her get out of bed every morning even after Donnie, the husband she'd adored, had been killed while serving in Afghanistan after they had been married for only an incredibly short two years. That was also the part that had decided to make her gather her courage together and to try to get to know her father's family.

The father who had, up until just recently, been a complete mystery in her life.

Ever since she could remember—until she'd gotten married—it had been just her mother and her. There had *been* no other family members to speak of, and that had been just fine with her. Filling in the blanks for herself, Chloe assumed that her father had been her mother's high school sweetheart who'd been killed in a car accident before he could marry her nineteen-year-old mother.

Because that had been her belief since forever, Chloe hadn't been prepared to learn that her father was actually tech giant Gerald Robinson. And even more, that for years now he'd been living under an assumed name. Gerald Robinson was in fact Jerome Fortune, one of the famous Texas Fortunes, no less. Neither had she been prepared for the eight legitimate Robinson offspring, giving her half siblings she'd never known she had.

And that didn't even begin to take into account the various illegitimate offspring the man had left scattered in his wake, as well.

All in all, it had been a great deal for her to take in and process.

Realizing that the man on the other end of the line, Graham Fortune Robinson, the third of Gerald's eight children, was still waiting for a response, Chloe answered quietly, "Yes, I'm still here."

Chloe could almost hear the pleased smile in her half brother's voice as he continued. "You might not remember me, but we met at that big family dinner at Kate Fortune's ranch."

How could she not remember? Chloe thought. She remembered everything about that evening, which had come about when Keaton Fortune Whitfield had contacted her out of the blue to tell her that he was her half sibling and invited her to come. And just like that, she'd gone from having no living relatives, now that her mother was gone, to having so many of them that she needed a scorecard just to keep track of them all.

She remembered how frightened and excited she'd been, walking into that huge mansion that evening. She'd harbored such great hopes.

Hopes that had been completely dashed when she'd met Sophie Fortune Robinson, her father's youngest daughter. At least his youngest *legitimate* daughter, Chloe silently amended. Everything had gone downhill from there when she'd introduced herself to Sophie. The latter had looked utterly appalled to meet her, and if looks could've killed, Chloe definitely wouldn't be alive to take this phone call right now.

Not that she could really blame Sophie, Chloe thought. It had to be quite a shock to find out that the man she had thought of as her father all those years had a completely other identity that she knew nothing about.

"Yes, I remember you," Chloe finally responded to Graham's comment.

She recalled that Graham had been the handsome, energetic young rancher and businessman whom Kate

Fortune had tapped to run Fortune Cosmetics for her. It was obvious that the reserved woman had been quite proud of him.

"I know this must seem strange, my calling you out of the blue like this," Graham said.

"No stranger than finding out after all these years that my father was Gerald Robinson," Chloe replied, wondering where all this was going.

After that family dinner, she would have bet that that was the last time she would ever see any of those people again. And, to be quite honest, the run-in with Sophie had left a bad taste in her mouth. She'd decided to keep her distance from the Fortunes, especially since her mother had never had an interest in reuniting with her father.

"If I remember correctly, you have a degree in counseling, don't you?" Graham was saying.

She was surprised that anyone even noticed her that night—other than thinking of her as an interloper. After all, how else would anyone regard their father's bastard child? Chloe thought ruefully.

"Yes, I do," she said uncertainly, waiting for Graham to get to the point—and wondering if, once he did, she was going to regret it.

"I know this might seem unusual to you," Graham continued.

Unusual doesn't begin to cover the half of it, Chloe thought.

"—but I'm calling with a job offer."

"A job offer?" Chloe echoed, stunned. "But you run Fortune Cosmetics. And I don't know anything about cosmetics, other than what I have in my medicine cabinet."

She heard Graham laugh. "You won't have to. Have you ever heard of Peter's Place?"

"Of course I've heard of it. That's a therapeutic ranch for troubled teenaged boys."

"Right." He sounded pleased with her answer. "Currently, my wife, Sasha, is the only counselor there. Because of a recent, rather generous donation from the Fortune Foundation, we're going to be expanding Peter's Place. I've been doing double duty running the ranch as well as helming Fortune Cosmetics. Frankly, between that and taking care of a baby plus our eight-year-old daughter, I'm spread pretty thin. I—we," he amended, including his wife, "could definitely use a bigger staff. Now, I realize that you're just starting out, but I've got a good feeling about you, Chloe. I'd like you to come down to Peter's Place for an interview—it'll pretty much just be a formality. And while you're here, you can take a look around the ranch—that is, if you're interested," he tagged on. It was clear from the way he spoke that he really hoped she was.

Life had robbed her of some of her optimism, making her suspicious of things that seemed to be too good to be true—which was why Chloe didn't immediately jump at the offer, the way she might have only a few years ago.

"Like you said, I'm just starting out. Why would you be offering this to me?" she wanted to know. "It sounds like you could hire anyone you wanted to."

"I know. And that's what I thought I was doing," he

told her. "I've made inquiries about you, Chloe. According to my sources, you're talented and you have a way with people. And," he added most significantly, "because you're family."

You're family.

Chloe felt a funny little sensation in the pit of her stomach. For most of her young life, it had been only her mother and her against the world. And then she'd married Donnie, only to have him taken from her all too soon two years ago. There was a part of her that was *starving* to be part of a family, even as part of her distrusted that feeling and the invitation she was being tendered.

Still, because there was that hunger to be part of something greater than just herself, to be accepted into a family, Chloe heard herself asking, "When would you like me to come down?"

Chapter One

Dear Lord, what am I doing?

The question echoed in her brain as Chloe pulled up before the main ranch house of Peter's Place.

Yes, she really wanted to be part of a family, part of this family, but did she really *want* to leave herself wide open like this? To get this close to the Fortunes? After all, she sternly reminded herself, her encounter last month with the clan was less than successful to say the least.

It all came vividly rushing back to her now as she turned off the ignition and sat quietly in the car for a moment.

She never should have agreed to this interview. She was too intimidated by Kate Fortune, the family matriarch, who Chloe figured would be at this meeting.

And why not? She seemed to run everything associated with the Fortune family.

Kate Fortune might well be ninety-one years old, but she looked decades younger and was sharp as the proverbial tack. The woman was not exactly the warm, cuddly grandmotherly type.

Was it too late to change her mind? Chloe thought not for the first time.

Then again, it wasn't as if she was exactly hip-deep in job offers, able to pick and choose which position she was willing to accept. Given that, this job that Graham was offering her was at least worth a look. Heaven knew she wasn't getting anywhere looking for work so far and she knew that Donnie wouldn't have wanted her to give up on life just because he was gone. And who knew? Maybe she'd actually get it and things would work out for the best.

There was always a first time, Chloe told herself philosophically, doing her best to bolster up her flagging courage.

"Well, here goes nothing," Chloe murmured under her breath as she unbuckled her seat belt and opened the door.

Glancing up into the rearview mirror before she exited the vehicle, she made one futile attempt to smooth down her wayward curly blond hair. Not that it did all that much good, she thought ruefully. Her hair seemed to have a mind of its own.

"Just like me," Chloe murmured, thinking of what her mother had often said.

You just keep dancing to your own drummer, Chloe. The world'll come around eventually to join you.

Satisfied that she looked as good as she was going to look on this crisp March day—the wind had seemed determined to restyle her hair the moment she'd stepped outside—Chloe got out of her sedan and closed the door.

She didn't bother locking the vehicle because it wasn't the kind of car that anyone would think to steal. It had already gone through several owners before she'd bought it a year ago. Close to ten years old, it ran mostly on faith and used parts.

Warning herself not to expect too much, Chloe went up the three steps to the ranch house front door. Mentally counting to ten as she took a deep breath and centered herself, she knocked on the door.

The second her knuckles made contact, the door seemed to fly open. As a matter of fact, she could have sworn that the door opened a second *before* she actually knocked on it.

But that had to be her imagination—right?

"Oh, Chloe, you're here," Graham said, looking startled to see her.

He wasn't in the doorway alone. Chloe recognized the pretty blue-eyed blonde right behind her half brother. It was his wife, Sasha. The petite woman looked even more frazzled than Graham did.

"I'm sorry. Did I get the dates mixed up?" Chloe asked, looking from Graham to his wife. It was the only conclusion she could draw, given the expressions on their faces and their almost breathless manner.

"No, no, you've got the right date," Graham assured

her. "But something's just come up. There's been a sudden family emergency. I just got a call from our babysitter that Maddie—that's our eight-year-old," he explained quickly, "decided that she'd give flying off the swing a try." He frowned, shaking his head. "It didn't turn out quite the way our fearless daughter had hoped. From all the screaming and crying, the sitter thinks that Maddie broke her arm. We're just on our way out to meet them at the hospital."

"Oh, I'm sorry," Chloe cried, genuinely concerned. She could just imagine what was going through their minds. But at least they had each other to lean on. "Is there anything I can do?"

It took him only a second to answer Chloe. "As a matter of fact, there is."

"What do you need?" she asked, ready to pitch in and help.

Chloe thought he was going to ask her to accompany him and his wife to whatever hospital their little girl had been taken. Maybe they were too rattled to drive safely. But that wasn't what he needed her to do.

"Would you mind sticking around for a while?" Graham asked her. "I've got someone else coming in for an interview and I couldn't reach him on the phone. I was going to call you as soon as we were on the road," Graham quickly explained. "When he gets here, tell him that as soon as I make sure that Maddie's all right, I'll be back. I know this is a huge imposition on you and I wouldn't ask if—"

"That's okay," Chloe said, cutting him off. She could tell just by his tone of voice that if he remained, the man's mind wouldn't be on the interview. "Go. See to your daughter." She all but shooed the couple out. "I'll stay."

"We won't forget this," Sasha promised, tossing the words over her shoulder as she and her husband rushed out of the house.

Chloe offered the couple an encouraging smile. "Glad to help," she called after them.

After all, it wasn't as if she was exactly pressed for time, Chloe thought, watching the duo get into their car and drive quickly away.

Besides, Chloe reasoned, walking back into the ranch house and closing the door behind her, this way she could get a look at whoever it was that she would be competing against for this job.

Chloe looked around. She liked the looks of the ranch from what she'd seen of it, driving up here. Maybe she was reading things into it, she thought, but it had a good feel about it.

Chloe sat down on the sofa, prepared to wait. She remained sitting for all of five minutes before she began to feel restless. On her feet again, she started to prowl around the large living room with its comfortable masculine furnishings.

Definitely a good feel to the place, she thought as she moved about, touching things and envisioning herself working here.

She looked at an old-fashioned clock with gold numbers on the fireplace mantel, and she could almost feel the minute hand dragging itself in slow motion, going from one number to the next.

How long was she expected to wait? If she'd had some sort of a handle on that, then she could put things into perspective—or at least know when it would be all right for her to leave.

The sound of a back door slamming made her jump. As did the sound of a wailing baby.

The next second, a rather beleaguered-looking older man came in, holding the crying baby in his arms and looking as if he was at his wit's end.

Without bothering to ask her who she was or to introduce himself, the man complained, "I can't get her to stop crying. I've tried everything and she just keeps right on bawling. Do you know how to make her stop?" he asked pathetically, holding the baby out to her like an offering. "Please?"

Chloe stared at the stranger, stunned. She didn't know the first thing about babies, and for all this man knew, she could have been some random thief who had just broken in to the house.

But he looked so distraught, she decided to skip pointing that out. Feeling sorry for the man, she said, "Give her to me," although, for the life of her, she had no idea what she was going to do.

"Thank you, thank you," the man cried. "This is Sydney. I'm Sasha's uncle Roger, by the way," he said as he placed the baby into her arms. "Graham and Sasha had an emergency and asked me to watch the baby while they were gone." He flushed, embarrassed. "I said yes before I knew what I was getting myself into. I thought the kid would stay asleep. But the second they were gone, she started crying." And then Roger stared at the infant, relieved and awestruck at the same time. "Hey, will you look at that," he marveled, looking from Sydney to the woman holding her. "She's really taken to you."

To Chloe's absolute amazement, the baby had stopped crying. She would have said there was some sort of magic involved, except it was obvious that Sydney appeared to be fascinated with the way the light was hitting the sterling silver pendant she was wearing around her neck.

The pendant that Donnie had given her just before he'd shipped out, she thought sadly.

Even now, you're still finding ways to help me out, Donnie.

"More like she's taken with my necklace," Chloe told Sasha's uncle.

To prove her point, she grasped the pendant and moved it around ever so slowly. Sunlight gleamed and shimmied along its surface. Sydney followed the sunbeam with her eyes, mesmerized.

"Hey, whatever it takes." Roger laughed. "I'm just really relieved that Sydney's finally stopped crying. I was afraid she was going to rip something loose inside that little body...or that I was going to start to lose my hearing. For a little thing, she's sure got a mighty big set of lungs on her."

For the first time, Roger turned his attention to Chloe. Apparently realizing that he didn't know who she was, he asked, "You a friend of Graham's and Sasha's?"

"Not exactly," Chloe replied.

She wasn't really sure how to introduce herself. Yes,

she was Graham's half sister, but she was still getting used to that title herself. She didn't know if she was comfortable enough to spring it on anyone else yet, not to mention that Graham might not welcome their connection becoming public knowledge.

Sitting down on the sofa as she continued to cradle and entertain the baby, Chloe evasively explained, "I'm here to interview for a job that's opened up at Peter's Place."

"Ah."

Roger nodded his head as he sat down, too. "Great place," he told her. "Sasha and Graham do a lot of good here. And they could certainly do with a few more willing hands to help them out with the work. You got a job in mind?" he asked.

"I'm applying for the counseling job," Chloe explained. Now that he was no longer distraught because he couldn't get the baby to stop crying, the older man seemed very easy to talk to.

"Counseling, huh? Like my niece."

She nodded. "Do you work at Peter's Place, too?" she wanted to know.

Roger's face registered surprise. "Me?" he cried, obviously stunned that she would think that. "No, I actually own the spread that Peter's Place sits on. The Galloping G Ranch," he told her proudly. "My house is down aways. I just came by when Graham and Sasha called, saying that they needed someone to watch Sydney here for a while. They forgot to tell me that I needed to bring my earplugs," he added with a laugh. "You don't mind my asking, how many kids have you got?"

"None," she replied, sincerely hoping that the pang she felt making that admission wasn't evident on her face.

She and Donnie had really wanted to start a family, but they had held off because Donnie was going overseas. He'd said that he wanted to be around while she was carrying his baby. Besides, he had told her, they had time. They had their whole lives in front of them.

Until they didn't, she thought sadly. She really wished he had gotten her pregnant before he left. At least she would have had a part of him to help her ease the pain of loss.

"I'm sorry. Did I say something to upset you?" Roger asked, clearly concerned.

Chloe shook her head. "No, I was just thinking of something."

"Oh, well, good. I wouldn't have wanted to upset you, especially since you've been such a help with Sydney here and all." He glanced at his watch, then looked up at her almost sheepishly. "Um, listen, I really need to make a phone call. Since Sydney here seems to really like you, would you mind holding her a bit longer while I make my call? Shouldn't be too long," he added.

The man was already edging his way toward the back of the house as he spoke. It was obvious that he was hoping she'd agree.

Chloe really wanted to hand the baby back to this man, but she couldn't very well turn down his request. Besides, she *had* promised Graham to wait until whoever he hadn't been able to reach on the phone turned up for his interview, so what was one more thing added to that?

"Sure, I can watch her," she told Roger.

The heavyset man beamed at her. "Thanks," he cried. "You're going to love working here. They're both really great people," Roger told her, giving her a quick fatherly pat on the shoulder just before he turned on his heel and quickly disappeared, leaving the same way he had entered.

"Looks like it's just you and me now, Sydney. I'm Chloe, by the way," she told the baby, who was staring up at her with enormous blue eyes, looking as if she was hanging on every word. "Your dad's half sister," she explained. "What's that?" Chloe pretended to lean in toward the baby to hear the "question" that Sydney had "asked."

"You didn't know he had a half sibling? Well, he does. Several of them from what I hear," she added with a laugh.

"Your grandfather really took that 'Be fruitful and multiply' passage in the Bible to heart, I guess. I've got a feeling that there's going to be lots of us popping up around here from now on. I hope when you start talking, Sydney, you're going to be good with names," she told the baby.

And then she smiled down at the sweet, innocent face that seemed to be listening to every word she said.

"You don't have a clue what I'm saying, do you?" Chloe asked and then laughed. "Know what? Maybe it's better that way. Maybe it'll all sort itself out by the time you're old enough to know what's going on. Until then—"

Chloe stopped talking abruptly when she heard someone knocking on the door.

Knowing it wouldn't be Graham and his wife, she figured it was the other candidate. *The one who's after my job.* She set her shoulders to do battle. "Let's go see if we can scare him off or talk him out of it, okay?"

Sydney made a little noise, and then the next moment Chloe saw that there were bubbles being formed around the infant's rosebud lips.

Chloe laughed, delighted. She shifted the baby, holding Sydney a little closer to her as she rose and began to head for the door.

"I'll take that as a yes," Chloe told the baby.

Sydney responded by making even more bubbles.

Chloe opened the door, but whatever greeting she had come up with to offer the person on the other side temporarily vanished.

This was *not* the type of person she had expected to see when she opened the door. Given the position that she assumed they were both competing for, Chloe had unconsciously thought that he'd be a rather scholarly-looking man. The kind who seemed to fade into the woodwork without anyone taking notice of him.

Instead, what she found herself looking at was a cowboy, most definitely an adrenaline-stirring cowboy. The kind whom women were given to fantasizing about whenever the word *cowboy* came up.

The man standing before her had to be about six foot three with shoulders wide enough to give him trouble getting through narrow doorways. He had somewhat unruly, dirty-blond hair and eyes so blue they looked as if they'd been cut right out of the sky. He was wearing tight jeans, a long-sleeved denim shirt, boots and a Stetson—set at what could only be described as a sexy angle. In summation, he looked picture-perfect.

If she had to guess, she would have said that the cowboy was somewhere in his late twenties.

What she didn't have to guess at was that the man was utterly gorgeous.

The second the thought occurred to her, it hit her with the force of a thunderbolt.

Gorgeous?

She hadn't even so much as *noticed* another man since Donnie had died, much less labeled that man as "gorgeous." What was happening here? she upbraided herself. Had she just lost her mind?

Chapter Two

Chance Howell realized that he wasn't just looking at the petite blonde holding the baby, he was actually staring at her. That couldn't be viewed as exactly getting off to a good start with who he assumed was the potential boss's wife. He'd gathered some background on Graham Fortune Robinson and knew the man had two kids, one of whom was an infant. Hence the logical leap.

"Um, excuse me," he began, feeling rather tongue-tied as he took off his hat and held it in his hands. "I'm Chance Howell. I've got an appointment with Graham."

"He's not here right now," the woman told him. "He was called away because of an emergency, but he wanted me to tell you that he'll be back soon."

"You must be Sasha. His wife," Chance added when the woman who was looking at him with large cornflower-blue eyes gave no indication that he had guessed her name correctly.

"What? Oh, no, no, I'm not. I'm Graham's half sister."

"Well, it's nice to meet you, 'Graham's half sister,'" Chance acknowledged, putting his hand out to her.

The woman shifted the baby to her other side so that she could shake hands with him.

"Chloe," she told him. "My name is Chloe. Chloe Elliott. And I guess we'll be interviewing for the same job once Graham gets back."

Chance could only stare at her. What was she, five-one, five-two? Did she say they were going to be competing for the same job? She didn't look like a rancher, and she certainly didn't look like any former military person he'd ever met. The ad he was answering was for a rancher, and it had said that preference would be given to any veterans who applied.

But then, what did he know? The world had been doing a lot of changing in these last few years. Black was white and white was black, and he'd heard that with proper drilling, tiny little ladies like her could mop the floor with guys like him.

That might even turn out to be an interesting experience, Chance caught himself thinking. The one thing he was certain of was that he was glad that the petite blonde wasn't married to the man who he hoped would be hiring him.

He glanced down at her hand, which she had tucked around the baby. It was still clearly visible for his purposes.

There was no wedding ring.

Maybe things were looking up, Chance mused. He could use a little good luck right about now.

"What branch of the service were you in?" he asked her, curious.

Chloe looked at him quizzically. "Service?" she repeated.

"Yeah, you know, navy, army, marines, air force. Service," he repeated. Had she been in some sort of secret branch? he wondered. Was that why she looked so reluctant to say anything?

"I wasn't in any branch," Chloe told him, looking bewildered. "What makes you think I was in the service?"

Aware he might have made a mistake, Chance backtracked. He didn't want to get off on the wrong foot by insulting the woman.

"Well, the ad said that preference would be given to veterans," he began, feeling as if he was on really shaky ground here.

"I didn't see the ad," she told Chance. "Graham just called to tell me about the position and he asked me to come out to the ranch to interview for it. And then he got called away because of that emergency."

He nodded. "Right. The emergency," he repeated. "So you said. Um, do you have any idea when he might be coming back?" He wasn't much for small talk, but this had to be a new low, even for him.

Chloe shrugged. "Not a clue. He just said he'd be back as soon as he could." She paused for a moment, as if searching for something to say in order to fill the stillness. "So, you served?" she asked.

Chance nodded. "Special Forces in Afghanistan—

until that IED sent me straight to the hospital, and eventually, stateside."

"Recently?" she asked, trying but failing to covertly scan his appearance.

The cowboy looked perfect, but she knew that there were some injuries and scars that weren't visible.

But in her opinion, the worst ones were the ones that didn't allow you to come home at all, other than in a coffin.

"No, I've been home for a few years now," Chance told her.

"Where's home?"

"Here and there," he answered vaguely. "I go wherever the work is." He didn't want it to sound as if the reason for his nomadic existence was because he didn't do a good job and was let go. "I don't stick around long in any one place," he confessed.

"Why? Are you looking for something?" Chloe asked.

"Not particularly."

It wasn't that Chance felt he was actually searching for something specific, he just stayed in one place until he began feeling restless. It was as if something inside him would suddenly tell him that it was time to go.

"I already know that the only place I ever feel like I'm at peace is on the back of a horse. I guess you could say that's my haven, my church," he explained.

She smiled at him, and it seemed to make its way to her eyes. "Lucky for you, you can keep your church close by so it's there whenever you need it."

He smiled back at her. "Something like that."

It wasn't really like that, but he wasn't about to

correct the blonde right off the bat. They hadn't even known each other for a total of five minutes yet. Correcting her wasn't exactly the way to get to know her any better.

He did, however, appreciate the fact that she wasn't grilling him, trying to make him explain his thinking. Some of the women he'd encountered would try to do just that—especially the ones who made it clear that they wanted him to stay with them.

Just as Chance was searching his mind for something to say, an older man burst into the living room.

Chloe looked at the older man in surprise. She'd completely forgotten he was in the house, making a call. "Did you finish making your call?"

He looked at her a little sheepishly. "It took longer than I thought," he apologized.

Obviously realizing that Chance had no idea who this man was, Chloe made the necessary introductions.

"Chance, this is Sasha's uncle Roger. Roger, this is Chance Howell. He's the other person Graham was going to interview today."

"The one he couldn't reach," Roger acknowledged, nodding his head as he shook hands with Chance. "Matter of fact, that's why I came back. Graham just called me to say that he and Sasha will be home soon. Looks like Maddie just broke her wrist, not her whole arm, but she's still got a big cast and from what I could tell, that is one unhappy eight-year-old," he added sympathetically.

"Anyway," Roger continued, addressing Chance, "Graham told me to tell you that you can reschedule your interview if you don't want to wait around until he gets in." He turned to Chloe. "Same goes for you if you're getting a mite antsy, waiting for him. Course, since you're so good with the baby and all, I'm hoping you'll stay."

"Sure, that's okay," Chloe told Sasha's uncle. "I'll stay until he gets here. No point in my going back and forth."

"Same here," Chance chimed in. His eyes met Chloe's and just for a moment, the job he had come out to apply for slipped into the background for him. "I'll be happy to stay."

What he really meant was that he was happy spending a little more time talking to the petite blonde with the sunbeam smile—even if talking didn't exactly come easy for him.

Chloe felt a quickening in the pit of her stomach. It was identical to the one she'd experienced when she'd first opened the door and caught sight of the tall, rangy-looking cowboy.

Careful, Chloe. Remember, been there, done that. You really don't want to go down that road again, do you? You know exactly where that road leads.

Donnie had been her first love. She'd fallen really hard for Donnie and had felt like jumping out of an airplane without strapping a parachute to her back. The feeling was nothing short of exhilarating, but in the end, leaping out of an airplane without a parachute was just asking for trouble, and that was the very last thing she wanted in her life: the kind of trouble that led directly to heartache.

But on the other hand, Chloe reasoned, she didn't

want to come across as rude, either, and being nice—cautiously nice—to Chance didn't hurt anything, she silently insisted.

The trick was that she had to remember not to get carried away.

Before she could say anything to him, Sasha's uncle stepped up.

"While you're waiting for Graham to get back," Roger offered, "I could give you two a tour of the place if you're interested."

"You mean of the house?" Chloe asked, looking down at the baby in her arms.

Sydney, to her surprise, had fallen asleep. Chloe had been so taken with the handsome cowboy, she hadn't even realized. Nor did she realize the pain in her shoulder till now. She didn't want to take a chance on waking the baby up, but on the other hand, she would really welcome the opportunity to set Sydney down in her crib.

"Well, the house to start with," Roger said, answering her question. "And then the rest of the ranch. I could take you two on a quick tour in my truck," he added in case they were worried about missing Graham when he and his wife returned.

Chloe looked down at the baby. "I don't want to risk waking Sydney up."

Roger looked as if he suddenly realized the position that Chloe was in.

"I guess I completely forgot about making you hold that little one," he confessed, embarrassed. He looked at Chance.

"It's up to you, Chloe," he said. "If you don't feel

comfortable about waking that little baby, we can stay right here and wait for Graham and his missus. I don't need special entertaining," he went on to tell her as he smiled. "I'm just fine the way I am."

You certainly are, Chloe thought.

The next minute, ashamed of herself, feeling guilty at being so flippant about Donnie's memory, she admonished herself for thinking that way. She really had to get hold of herself. What was wrong with her? This wasn't like her at all.

"I don't want to keep you from seeing the ranch," she protested, ready to wave Chance and Roger off on their way.

"If I get the job, I'll be seeing it soon enough," Chance told her. "And if I don't get the job, well then, there's really no point in taking a tour around the place, now is there?"

Roger looked a little perplexed as he listened to the exchange between the two younger people. Lifting his somewhat sloping shoulders, he shrugged and then let them fall again.

"Suit yourselves," he told them. "But meanwhile, I can show you where Sydney's room is so you can at least put her down in her crib. That way you can see if you can still move your arms." Turning, Roger beckoned for her to follow. "It's this way, Chloe."

She saw no reason not to do that, as long as she could hear the baby if she started crying again. She was fairly confident that there had to be a baby monitor in Sydney's room.

Feeling a sense of relief that she'd at least be away

from Chance for a minute or two—enough time to break whatever spell he'd seemed to cast over her—Chloe happily fell into step behind Sasha's uncle.

"Guess I might as well come, too," Chance said to them. "No sense in standing around, talking to myself."

Oh, joy. Just what she needed. More of the handsome cowboy.

Chapter Three

Chloe eased the baby ever so slowly into the crib. She held her breath the entire time until she was able to successfully withdraw her hands from around the baby's little body.

Sydney made a little noise, then sighed before settling back to sleep.

Success! Chloe silently congratulated herself.

She took a step back and almost gasped as she bumped up right against Chance.

"Oh, sorry," he whispered, immediately moving aside. He wasn't sure if he was apologizing for being in her way or for feeling that sudden zip of electricity surging through his body when it made contact with hers. Granted the contact wasn't of the intimate variety that he was normally accustomed to, but there was still just enough to get him going.

Chloe instantly turned around and nearly caused another, far more dead-on collision between them. At the very last minute, because Chance had moved back so quickly, the one-on-one collision between their two bodies was avoided.

She wasn't really sure if she was relieved—or perhaps just a little disappointed.

Again? What is the matter with you? she silently demanded.

Yes, the man was attractive, she acknowledged, but lots of men were attractive and she hadn't been drawn to them. So why was this man, this *cowboy*, different from the others?

He's not. Get a grip, Chloe, she ordered herself angrily.

"Um, that's okay." She flushed, absolving him of any guilt in what had just transpired. "I shouldn't have moved so suddenly." She looked down at the sleeping infant. "I just didn't want to take a chance on saying something too loud and waking up the baby."

Since the room was relatively small, Roger had kept back, standing almost out in the hallway. He peered in now at the sleeping infant.

"She sure is a pretty little thing, ain't she?" The whispered rhetorical question was steeped in complete admiration. And then he looked from Chance to Chloe. "You got any kids?" he asked Chance.

The cowboy looked surprised by the question. "No."

"You already told me that you don't have any," Roger

said to Chloe. And then he laughed to himself, as if he knew something they weren't privy to yet. "Well, you two are young yet. You've got time."

Time—that was what Donnie had thought. They had time. Time to be together, time to enjoy one another before they took that step to become parents. Again she wished with all her heart she had insisted on getting pregnant before he had left for overseas. At least she would have had Donnie's child to hold in her arms instead of all that emptiness that he left behind.

"But once you've got 'em," Roger was saying, "there's just nothing like it in the world. Makes you realize just what you were put down here on earth for, what makes everything else all worthwhile." Rousing himself, he beckoned them out into the hallway. "C'mon, we'd better slip out before I forget myself and start talking loud again."

Roger put a hand on each of their shoulders—he had to stretch in order to reach Chance's—and he guided them both out ahead of him.

The hallway was too narrow to accommodate all three of them. Roger fell behind them again.

As she and Chance fell in step beside each other, he glanced her way. "You want kids?" he asked her out of the blue as they made their way back down the stairs ahead of their unofficial escort.

"Right now, I just want a job," she told him honestly. The next second, she realized that he might think she was trying to guilt him out of competing for the position he was here for. "I mean, if I turn out to be more qualified for it. But if it turns out that you are, well then, I'll just have to keep on looking for something," she concluded.

Chance caught himself studying her. Something just wasn't adding up for him.

"Just how much do you know about ranching?" he finally asked her.

Reaching the bottom of the stairs, she stared at him, confused. Why would he ask her such a strange question? "Not much. Why?"

Something's really *not adding up*, Chance told himself. "Well, because that's the job I'm here about. The one I'm interviewing for. Graham wanted someone to run the ranch. Someone who was good with horses," he finally said when she just kept looking at him.

"Run the ranch?" Chloe repeated, confused. She'd gotten the impression from Graham that she and Chance were here about the same job. She looked at him now. "You're here about ranching?"

"Funny, I thought I just said that," Chance answered. Judging by the expression on her face, she *wasn't* here to apply for that job the way she'd made it sound earlier. "What are you here about?"

"Why, counseling, of course," Chloe replied in no uncertain terms.

"Counseling what?" Chance asked, clearly surprised by her answer. And then it suddenly occurred to him what the sexy-looking blonde was saying. He had to admit that what he'd just asked made him feel like an idiot. "You mean the boys?"

Her smile was a natural reflex. "I kind of have to. Horses don't listen to me."

Chloe's sense of humor tickled him and he laughed. Now it all made sense. They were here about two different positions. "I could teach you how to make them listen to you."

"You're talking about the horses, right?" she asked, a hint of mischief dancing in her eyes.

He found himself being pulled in and mesmerized by those deep pools of blue. It took effort to tear his gaze away. "Right," he finally replied. "I've got no trouble getting horses to listen to me. Most people, though, just ignore me like I wasn't there."

"I don't believe that for a minute," she told him with feeling. How could *anyone*, male or female—especially female—not notice this man? His presence seemed to just fill up the very space around him. Heaven knew he certainly did that for her.

The way he was looking at her right now made her feel like nervously shifting from foot to foot. The butterflies in her stomach were multiplying at a phenomenal rate. It was hard to gather her thoughts together to answer him.

"For one thing, you're really tall." She knew that wasn't much of an answer, so she searched for a better one. "And you have this commanding air about you. If you *were* a counselor, I'm sure that the boys here would listen to whatever you had to say."

"Good thing we won't have to put that to the test," Chance answered, then confessed, "I'm not much when it comes to giving orders. I had enough of that when I was over in Afghanistan."

The mention of the place that had seen Donnie die had her quietly saying, "At least you got to come back."

The words slipped out before she could think to stop them. Any hope that Chance might not have heard her died the second she looked up into his eyes. He'd heard. There was curiosity mingled with a touch of pity in his blue orbs.

The moment grew more uncomfortable for her.

"Did you lose someone?" Chance asked kindly.

Her first impulse was to deny his assumption. But that would be like denying Donnie had ever existed, and she couldn't bring herself to do that.

So after a couple of beats had gone by, she answered him. "Yes."

"Brother? Father? Husband?" Chance kept guessing when she made no acknowledgment that he had guessed correctly. By the time he'd reached the word *husband*, with no visible response from her, Chance shook his head. "No, never mind. Don't tell me. It's none of my business. Sorry I asked," he apologized. "It's just that sometimes it feels like some kind of exclusive veterans club—the kind you really don't want membership to," he added ruefully.

"Does that mean you wish you hadn't gone?" she asked, curious.

How many times had she lain awake at night, wondering if Donnie ever regretted enlisting before the war had taken him from her. Even now, after all this time, she hadn't really come to any sort of a satisfactory conclusion.

"No," he told her honestly. "I went to fight for my

country, and I'm proud of that part. I just wish I hadn't seen what I'd seen. Nobody should see that kind of thing," he said quietly. "Nobody should have to live through it, either."

Then, as if he replayed his own words in his head, Chance blew out a breath, mystified. "How'd I get started on that?" he asked. The question was meant more for him than for her. Clearing his throat, he abruptly changed the subject. "Anyway, at least now we know that we're not out for the same job."

Roger, who had been hanging back quietly this whole time, finally spoke up.

"Well, glad that's been cleared up—and just in time, too." His attention was immediately redirected to the sound of the front door being opened. "Looks like your future bosses are back," he told Chloe and Chance with a broad wink.

They turned toward the front door in time to see Graham and Sasha walking in, along with a little girl. With her straight blond hair and her delicate features, she looked like a miniature version of her mother. All except for the arm that was in a cast and held by a sling around her neck.

Chloe winced in sympathy. That had to be Maddie, she thought, her heart immediately going out to the little girl. She hoped that Maddie wasn't in too much pain.

"Well, we made it back," Sasha announced. "Sorry for the wait." She looked around. "Uncle Roger, where's the baby?"

Roger pointed to Chloe. "This one got her to go to sleep just like that." He snapped his fingers to illustrate just how fast Chloe had performed what was clearly a magic trick to him.

Sasha smiled warmly at Chloe.

"Well, I'm won over. You've got the job," Sasha quipped.

"You're not serious, are you?" Chloe asked uncertainly.

"No, she's not," Graham agreed. "But almost," he told Chloe. "Sasha goes on gut instincts, same as me," he told her.

"Hey, kiddo, you want to go upstairs and lie down?" Roger asked his grandniece, who had momentarily gotten lost in this verbal exchange between the adults.

"No," Maddie cried, protesting the very idea. "They had me lying down forever when I was in the hospital, getting all those pictures took of my arm." She looked at her cast. "What I want is you to sign my cast," she declared, pointing to the newly applied cast with her other hand. Barely an hour old, the cast already had a handful of autographs and well-wishes written on it. "I got these from the nurses. And that's from that doctor who put it on," she told her granduncle, pointing out the different signatures. "Isn't it neat?"

"It sure is," Roger agreed with the kind of enthusiasm that appealed to young children. "Neatest thing I've ever seen. What do you say you and me go get us a sandwich in the kitchen and I'll see if I can come up with something real good to put on that cast?"

Maddie perked up visibly. "Can I have anything I want to eat?" she asked eagerly.

"You can have anything that's in the refrigerator," Roger qualified with a wink.

Maddie's grin all but split her face. "Cool!"

Roger pretended to misunderstand her declaration. "Cool or hot. Whatever's there, is yours."

Sasha exchanged looks with her amused husband. "I think maybe I should go supervise," Sasha said, following her uncle.

Wanting to be as accommodating as possible, Chloe called out after Sasha's departing back, "I'll just sit right here until you get back."

"You can if you want to, but feel free to move around if you like. You've already got the job," Sasha called back over her shoulder, accompanying her injured daughter to the kitchen.

Chloe looked at Graham. Sasha hadn't asked her a single question that had to do with the job she was applying for. Just what had gotten the woman to decide in her favor?

"I'm confused," Chloe confessed.

He laughed. "Sasha'll do that to you," he said in a completely understanding voice. "I feel like my head's been spinning ever since I first met her. But since she's a better judge than I am when it comes to this position, I've made up my mind. You do have the job." And then he grew more serious. "Do you mind being left alone for a few minutes?" he asked. "I'd like to ask Chance some questions in private."

Then, before she could answer him, he made a suggestion. "Feel free to look around the house, or to join Sasha, Maddie and Uncle Roger in the kitchen."

Chloe shook her head, declining both offers. Right now, she just wanted to sit exactly where she was and absorb what had just happened.

And, in her opinion, what had just happened amounted to being given a job, a rather important job in her estimation, practically sight unseen.

Well, she'd been seen, Chloe amended, but obviously a great deal had just been read into whatever Sasha Fortune Robinson *thought* she saw in her.

"I'm good, thank you," she told Graham, turning down his offer.

In response, her half brother smiled at her and nodded. "I won't be long," he promised.

Her half brother.

It was still hard to think of him that way, Chloe thought as she watched him take Chance into what appeared to be a den that was directly off the living room.

Hard to think of herself as being anyone's half sister.

Or a half sister to what amounted to practically a legion of other half siblings, she added silently. She'd grown up thinking she had no family at all beyond her mother and now she had more family than she could shake that proverbial stick at.

And one of those half siblings had just given her a job.

Not just *any* job but the kind of job she had set her heart on before she'd ever sent in her application to college. So far, she'd been stitching together a living taking anything she could get—even working at a local coffee shop on weekends to help pay her rent. She felt as if she'd finally crossed a threshold into her field.

Talk about luck.

Glancing around to make sure no one could see her, Chloe pinched herself. And then, just to make certain, she pinched herself again because she had to admit this all seemed like some sort of dream. A dream that she was going to wake up from at any minute now.

Except for the part about Donnie, she thought grimly. If this *was* a dream, he'd be right here beside her.

But he wasn't.

She was sitting in this big old living room all by herself, waiting for her half brother to come back in and tell her all the details she needed to know about this job she was going to be starting. She was convinced that she'd gotten this position strictly because she was "family" despite all of Graham's talk about instincts and gut feelings.

No matter, she was determined to prove to them that they hadn't made a mistake in hiring her. She was going to work really, really hard and be the best counselor they could have possibly hoped for. She owed it to them.

Most of all, she owed it to herself—and to the memory of her husband, who had always encouraged her and told her she could be absolutely anything she wanted to be once she set her mind to it.

She glanced toward the door that Graham had closed behind him and Chance. She wondered how the interview was going.

She really hoped that Chance was going to get the job. She'd gotten the impression that although Chance wasn't down on his luck, landing this position at Peter's Place was really important to him.

Without realizing it, Chloe crossed her fingers for him, wishing that she was one of those people who actually believed in sending good vibes. Because if she was, she'd be sending them right now.

She watched the door intently.

And when it finally opened, only a few minutes later, she popped to her feet like a newly refurbished jack-in-the-box. Fingers still crossed, her eyes immediately went to the taller of the two men emerging from the room.

Chance was smiling.

She was confident that she knew the results before he said a word.

Chapter Four

Chance's smile was as broad as his shoulders as he crossed to her.

"Looks like you turned out to be my good-luck charm," he told Chloe. "'Cause I got the job."

"Luck has nothing to do with it," Graham told him, reaching up just a little to put his hand on his newest ranch hand's shoulder. "The people you worked for all spoke very highly of you. As a matter of fact, Kyle Mc-Masters said to tell you that if it doesn't work out for you here, he'd be more than happy to have you come back to work for him at the Double M."

Chance made no comment regarding his former boss's remark. Instead, he looked at his new boss and asked, "When can I start?"

"Bright and early tomorrow morning'll be fine." As

a rule, ranch hands were usually up around sunrise, if not before, so Graham made a suggestion. "How does seven o'clock suit you?"

The early hour didn't faze him in the slightest. He was accustomed to being up earlier, even when he wasn't working. It was just the way his inner clock worked. "I can be here earlier if you need me to be," Chance told him.

"No, seven'll do fine. You can bring your gear then and move in to the bunkhouse," Graham told him. "We've got two on the premises. One just for the ranch hands and the other one's where the boys stay."

"Sounds good to me," Chance replied. "All I really require is enough space to stretch out at the end of the day, nothing more."

Graham nodded. "We're going to get along just fine," he predicted. "Just to let you know, I've got plans for you. You're not just going to be a ranch hand. After you get the lay of the land around here, and things look like they're going well, I want to make you the coordinator for Peter's Place."

Graham smiled. "I think your being ex-military might just come in handy. The boys who are here now need a firm hand and they need to be made to respect authority. That's not to say I want you coming down hard on them. Just make sure they don't take advantage of you or anyone else here," Graham added. He looked deliberately at Chloe as he said the last part.

Chloe appreciated the thought, but she had been looking after herself for a long time now.

"You don't have to worry about me," Chloe told her

half brother. "I might not be as tall as you two, but I'm not a pushover, either. And I can definitely take care of myself."

Graham held up a hand. "I never meant to imply that I thought of you as a pushover. But knowing someone has your back certainly doesn't hurt in this kind of a situation," Graham assured her.

Then he launched into a rundown of the current residents staying at Peter's Place. "Right now, we've got four boys staying here. They're all decent kids, but for one reason or another, they've lost their way and all of them feel like they've been dealt a pretty bad hand." He spared a glance at Chloe. "Sasha can do a better job filling you in," he said to Chloe.

As if on cue, his wife came in from the kitchen. "Did I just hear my name being mentioned?" she asked, a bright smile on her face. Before Graham had an opportunity to respond to her question, Sasha told her husband, "You'll be happy to know that breaking her wrist did not affect our daughter's appetite. She's eating up a storm in there. Uncle Roger's whipping up his 'famous' corn dogs wrapped in bacon for her. I set the limit at two but I've got a feeling he's not going to stick to that. Maybe you can make him understand the wisdom of not letting Maddie stuff herself to the gills."

"I'm on it," Graham said, beginning to leave the living room.

Sasha looked at Chance and Chloe. "So, I take it that they both said yes."

"That they did," Graham said, tossing the words over his shoulder.

"Well then, welcome to Peter's Place," Sasha told the duo warmly. "I hope you like it here," she added. "We try to keep it homey. For some of these boys, this is the first actual 'home' they've had in quite a while."

The sound of a baby crying was heard coming over the monitor that Chloe had positioned on the wide coffee table.

Sasha sighed wearily as she looked at the monitor. "Looks like I'm being summoned," she told Chloe as she started to get up.

"Why don't you stay here and get Chloe up to speed on the boys who are currently here?" Graham suggested. Sasha began to point out the obvious, but never got very far. "I'll go see to Sydney," Graham told her. "I'm sure Uncle Roger knows enough not to overfeed Maddie. If he doesn't, Maddie's got enough sense to stop." Pausing for just a moment before he went up the stairs, he turned toward Chance. "And I'll see you in the morning."

"Count on it," Chance told him. Putting his Stetson on, he tipped it ever so slightly to the right, unaware that he was creating a rakish image as he did so. Chance nodded first at Graham's wife and then at Chloe. "Ladies, I'll see you tomorrow," he promised just before he headed for the door.

Chloe just stared at his retreating form. A very sexy form, she had to admit.

"He's a tall one, don't you agree?"

The comment snapped Chloe to attention. She hadn't even realized she was still staring at the closed door.

"What? Oh, you mean Chance. Yes, I guess he is at that," she murmured.

When she looked at Sasha, she thought she saw a hint of a grin on her lips. She hoped that Sasha didn't think that there was anything between her and Chance—or that there would be in the future. She'd come here strictly because she wanted work as a counselor and nothing more, she silently insisted.

"So tell me about the boys at Peter's Place," Chloe urged. She thought it best to change the subject immediately.

Sasha sat down beside her on the sofa, and then a sudden thought occurred to her. "Oh, where are my manners? Having your daughter break her wrist kind of knocks everything else out of your head," she apologized, then asked, "Can I get you anything? Something to drink perhaps?"

Chloe shook her head. She didn't want anything to distract her. Right now, all she wanted to do was focus on any information that Sasha could give her. She wanted to be as fully prepared as possible when she finally met the boys who had been sent here to atone for their misdeeds and to ultimately become better people.

"No, I'm fine. Really," she stressed when Sasha looked at her somewhat skeptically. "Just tell me about the boys I'm going to be working with. I want to learn all I can about them."

Sasha seemed to ponder her reply for a moment, no doubt wanting to cite the boys in the proper order.

Then she began. "The first teen we took in here at Peter's Place is Jonah Wright. A basically good boy,

Jonah kind of hit a rough patch when his father ran off, deserting the family. Consequently, to make ends meet, his mother had to hold down two jobs. Because she wasn't home very much, she expected Jonah to look after his three younger siblings. I don't have to tell you that that's a lot of responsibility to heap on such young shoulders. Jonah loved playing baseball after school and he had to give that up in order to be there for his siblings.

"After a while, life felt as if it was crashing in on him and Jonah just kept getting angrier and angrier. He started ditching school, vandalizing property and getting into fights almost all the time. He started shoplifting and got away with it the first couple of times.

"And then he got arrested. They were going to send him to jail, then at the last minute, the authorities decided to send him here instead. It was kind of touch and go with Jonah for a while, but he turned things around and it looks like he's on the road to getting his life back." Sasha smiled, clearly pleased to be able to relate this to Chloe. "Things look pretty promising and he's even going to be playing baseball soon, just like he always wanted to."

Sasha stopped for a moment, seeming to gather her thoughts.

"The second teen who was sent here was Ryan Maxwell. He was a lot less hostile than Jonah was when he came here, but he was also a great deal more depressed and withdrawn."

"Do you know why he was depressed?" Chloe wanted to know.

Sasha nodded. "Both of his parents died and social services sent him to live with his uncle. Family isn't always the best way to go," Sasha told her. "In Ryan's case, his uncle turned out to be a lowlife. He stole and spent all of the money that Ryan's parents had set aside to pay for his college education. Personally, I suspect that Ryan got into trouble and vandalized private property just to get away from the man."

"You're probably right," Chloe agree. "He probably felt he had nothing to lose and just maybe something to gain if he got away from his uncle."

Sasha smiled. "Since he came here, he's been doing a lot better. He's now in both a math club *and* a science club in school. If he keeps things up this way, he's on track to get a college scholarship," Sasha told her proudly. "And if that happens, he can write his own ticket. His future is a great deal more promising than his past."

"And the other boys?" Chloe asked, wondering if their stories would wind up ending this well.

"Well, the last two are newer and I'm afraid they haven't really adjusted to living here—yet," Sasha emphasized, obviously holding out a great deal of hope for the fates of both of these newer residents at Peter's Place. "Brandon Baker lost his older brother in Afghanistan, and I get the distinct feeling that he's just mad at the whole world right now."

Chloe could certainly identify with the way Brandon felt. When Donnie had been killed, there was a point when she'd been convinced that her anger was going to suffocate her. It had been touch and go for a while.

"And the last boy?" Chloe prompted.

"That would be Will Sherman. His mother is a single parent, and she has her own share of problems. The woman is an alcoholic," Sasha confided. "The Dr. Jekyll/Mr. Hyde kind who takes all of her frustrations out on Will. A social worker found him wandering the streets one night, so battered she didn't know how he was able to even stand up, much less walk." Tears shone in Sasha's eyes as she told Chloe, "When the social worker questioned him, he denied that his mother had beaten him. It was heartbreaking how protective he was of that woman. But it was obvious to everyone who came in contact with this boy that he couldn't be allowed to go back home. It was just as obvious that it would be just a matter of time before Will turned to less than acceptable ways, trying to support himself on the street.

"He's been here for a while, and I think he still feels that life has abandoned him, just like his mother has. He needs to learn how to relate to people and how to trust again."

Finished with her brief summation, Sasha paused and looked at Chloe. "Well, have I managed to scare you off yet?"

Chloe didn't have to hunt for words in order to answer her. As far as she was concerned, what Sasha had just outlined was her mission in life. Helping boys like the ones she spoke of.

"No, of course not. It's obvious that all these boys need help, and that's what I'm here for. What kind of a counselor would I be if I turned tail and ran at the first sign of a problem?"

"Possibly one who slept better at night?" Sasha suggested, a hint of a smile playing on her lips.

"The exact opposite," Chloe contradicted with feeling. "I wouldn't be able to sleep, knowing I didn't even try to help these boys. That I'd failed to reach out to them. Nobody deserves to have their dreams shattered the way these boys have, or to have their mothers beat them every time they descend into an alcoholic stupor."

Chloe knew the sort of first impression she made and the image that she projected when people first met her. She made people think of a sweet Girl Scout selling cookies door-to-door. But she wasn't interested in selling cookies.

"Believe me," she said, "I know life isn't all milk and cookies, but it shouldn't be all pain and sorrow, either."

As she spoke, Chloe could feel that she was really getting into the spirit of this new job she was about to undertake. She also felt she had a lot to offer.

"I know what it's like to grow up without a father and be raised by a single mother. I know what it's like to have to do without things other kids have, and I *definitely* know what it's like to lose someone and how that can cut right into your very soul." Her eyes met Sasha's, determination shining in them. "I think I can really help these boys," Chloe told her sister-in-law with fierce feeling.

Sasha beamed at her as she took the woman's hands in hers.

"I think you can, too," she said. "And I'm really glad Graham suggested that we hire you." She let go of Chloe, then tilted her head as if in thought for a moment. Then she said, "You know, we have an extra bedroom right here in the house. It might be easier for all of us if you lived here, on the premises."

Chloe hesitated, which prompted Sasha to quickly make another suggestion.

"We also have a small guest cottage on the property right behind the house. Now that I think of it, that might be more to your liking. You'd still be on the premises, but there wouldn't be that feeling of having Graham and me breathing down your neck," she added with an understanding smile.

"Oh, no, I wouldn't feel that," Chloe protested.

She didn't want to insult either Sasha or her half brother. They had gone out of their way to reach out to her while the others hadn't. That meant a great deal to her. She doubted that either one of them could begin to understand how much this new connection—being part of the family—meant to her. She was thrilled and excited about it and didn't want to do anything that would make them regret bringing her into the fold.

"Well, I'd feel that way in your place," Sasha said quite honestly. Her eyes met and held Chloe's. "Chloe, I have just one real hard-and-fast rule," she told the younger woman. "Always tell me the truth. No matter how you think hearing it might affect me, *always* tell me the truth. This way I won't have to wonder if you're being honest with me, or if you're just trying to spare my feelings."

Chloe took a breath. "Okay, this is me being honest. Yes, I can see how having me live here would be more beneficial so I could be on call anytime for the boys, and yes, I would rather have my own small space than live in the main house with you. That way, I won't be underfoot," she added.

Sasha laughed, looking pleased at the progress they seemed to be making. "There now, was that so hard?"

"Actually, yes," Chloe admitted. When Sasha raised her eyebrow quizzically, she explained, "I don't like worrying that I might be hurting people's feelings."

"Well, I for one would rather have my feelings hurt than find out I have been lied to—even if it involves just a little white lie," Sasha added with a wink. "All right, it's settled," she announced, rising to her feet. "You'll be moving in to the guest cottage," she told the other woman. "It hasn't been used for a while, so if there's anything you find that you need—or that needs fixing— please don't hesitate to tell either Graham or me.

"While I have to admit that we aren't exactly the handiest people in the world, we do have the connec- tions to always find someone who is." Again, she took Chloe's hands in hers. "We want you to be happy here," she told Chloe.

"Just being given the opportunity to try to help those boys you told me about will make me happy," Chloe responded.

"Good, I'm glad." Sasha released her hands. "But don't expect miracles," she warned. "This isn't some TV drama where everything's tied up neatly with a big red bow and fixed in sixty minutes—not counting com- mercials," Sasha added flippantly.

"I know that," Chloe assured her. "I have a degree in counseling, not fantasy."

"As long as we're on the same page," Sasha said agreeably.

Just as Chloe rose to leave, Graham came in carrying Sydney. The baby was crying just the same way she had when Chloe had first encountered her.

"What's wrong, little one?" Sasha asked her daughter.

"I'm not sure. I changed her and I don't think she's hungry. Uncle Roger said that she was screaming her lungs out earlier, until Chloe—" he nodded at his half sister "—got her to stop."

"Chloe?" Sasha asked, looking at the other woman with interest.

"All I did was just hold her when he handed her to me," Chloe said, not about to take credit for any sort of "miracle."

The next thing she knew, Graham was handing the baby over to her.

Startled, she took the baby and after a few seconds of rocking, Sydney stopped crying again.

Sasha looked on, clearly surprised and very pleased. "Maybe we should offer you two jobs here at Peter's Place," she quipped.

Graham exchanged looks with his wife. "Works for me," he chimed in.

In response to their words, Chloe felt a warm feeling spreading out all through her. A feeling of acceptance.

She blinked several times to keep the tears back.

Chapter Five

"Looks like today's moving day for both of us," Chance observed the next day, peering into the guesthouse through the door that Chloe had left opened.

Startled, Chloe swung around, her hand pressed against her pounding heart, to find the tall cowboy standing just outside the doorway. Naturally assuming that she was alone, she had just begun arranging the furnishings in her new quarters to her liking.

The guesthouse was actually more of a large studio apartment with a small bathroom attached to it than an actual house in the traditional sense. But located about a hundred yards behind the main house, it felt like her own private little space, which was all that really mattered to Chloe right now. It made her part of the whole organization, yet just separate enough to satisfy her need to be alone at times.

Except that right now, she wasn't alone.

"Hey, I didn't mean to scare you," Chance apologized, crossing the threshold. "I guess I should make more noise when I come up behind someone."

Embarrassed at her reaction—he was probably going to think she was afraid of her own shadow—Chloe waved away the cowboy's apology.

"No, I was just really focused on trying to figure out where to put my things." She glanced around again. Somehow, with Chance inside, the space looked smaller to her than it had a few minutes ago. "I think I brought too much with me. I just wasn't sure what I was going to need."

He'd seen a sedan parked by the guesthouse. There were a number of boxes and a couple of suitcases in the backseat.

"You have a place of your own apart from here?" he asked. Sometimes he forgot that most people did. He'd moved around so much since he'd been discharged from the army that when he was in between jobs, he just lived out of his truck. It was simpler that way.

Chloe nodded. "An apartment in town." It wasn't all that big—but it was bigger than the guesthouse, she thought.

Usually one to keep to himself, Chance realized he was asking too many questions, but curiosity was spurring him on. "If you've already got a place, why aren't you staying there? Can't be that far away from the ranch," he guessed.

"Sasha thought it might be easier if I was on the premises to begin with. You know, just in case there was some kind of an emergency with one of the boys, they wouldn't have to wait for me to drive in." Replaying her words in her head, Chloe laughed. "I guess that sounds kind of dramatic, doesn't it?" She supposed she could have just told Sasha that she could make the run from her apartment to the ranch quickly enough if the need arose. "It's just that this is my first real counseling job and I don't want anything to go wrong."

She saw a look akin to sympathy enter Chance's piercing blue eyes. "Oh, it'll go wrong," he said with certainty.

This wasn't the sort of pep talk she'd expected, Chloe thought. As a matter of fact, it sounded more like some kind of prediction of doom.

She stared at him. "What?"

Maybe he should have explained what he meant when he said that, Chance thought. "No matter how perfect things are, something is always bound to go wrong. It doesn't have to be some kind of a major disaster—and it usually isn't," he said with certainty. "But it's a fact of life that things do go wrong, usually when you least expect them to. Once you make your peace with that, you can relax and get the job done," he told her. "Just remember, do the best you can. Nobody expects perfection."

Easy for you to say, she thought. *Just look at yourself.*

"Do things go wrong for you?"

What he'd just said made her curious. She imagined that Chance was quite good at what he did. Practice alone probably made him perfect, and from what she'd gathered from Sasha, Chance had worked on ranches both before and after his stint in the military.

He laughed, tickled by the fact that she actually thought he might say no.

"Do you want that alphabetically, chronologically or listed in order of importance? And if it's the last one, would you like that in descending order or ascending order?"

Realizing that maybe she'd made a mistake, Chloe put her hands up as if to ward off any further questions.

"Point taken," she told Chance.

Looking at him more closely, she decided that he looked pretty relaxed. Since he'd mentioned something about it being "moving day" for both of them, she assumed that Chance had finished moving in to the bunkhouse. Men always had less baggage than women, she thought enviously. "I guess you're all settled in."

Chance moved his shoulders in a careless shrug. "A couple of changes of clothing, an extra pair of boots, razor, shaving cream and toothbrush. Not exactly much to 'settle,'" he told her, going through everything he'd brought with him.

Chance looked around the guesthouse. There was a combination stove, refrigerator and sink unit against one wall with a table for two right in front of it. Next to that was a sofa that he suspected pulled out into a bed. It was facing a small flat-screen on the wall that looked as if it was the latest piece of technology. Near the flat-screen was a chest of drawers.

It seemed like almost too much space for him, he thought.

"Need help with anything?" he asked her.

She'd already gotten started. "I just need to bring in a couple of suitcases and three boxes from my car. Oh, and I picked up two bags of groceries on my way here. But now that I see the size of the refrigerator, I'm not sure if it'll all fit in there."

"You could always stash the excess in the closet," Chance suggested with a straight face.

"I could," she allowed, taking his suggestion at face value. "If it was a walk-in. But it's not. It's barely a hang-in," she quipped.

His eyebrows drew together as he tried to make sense out of what she'd just said. "A what?"

She flushed just a little. "That was a lame joke about there not being enough room to hang more than a handful of clothes in the closet."

That had never been a problem for him. "I never really had more than a handful of clothes at any one time myself."

That fit the image she'd gotten of him. "Of course you didn't. Just your cowboy hat, your boots and your lariat should cover it," she deadpanned.

His eyes crinkled a little in amusement. "You been peeking into my closet, Chloe Elliott?"

The thought of peeking into his living space suddenly made her blush. She struggled to get that under control. "Just making an educated guess."

He wondered if he seemed that predictable to her, or if she was just kidding. Either way, she struck him as a fairly sharp lady. "Well, if that's the kind of thing a degree in counseling gets you, I'd say that it was money well spent."

That being said, he had to admit he was a little leery of psychologists and people who felt all problems could be tackled and solved by delving deeply into people's backgrounds and into what made them tick. That meant hours and hours of talking. He believed in action, not in talking a thing to death.

"But just so you know," he added, "I don't really enjoy having someone poking around in my head, wanting to know if I grew up thinking there were monsters under my bed."

"I don't blame you," she agreed so readily, he found himself believing her. "Neither do I."

Chance jerked a thumb toward the car she had parked out front. "Want me to bring in those suitcases and boxes for you?"

She didn't want him feeling as if he had to do anything for her. And she didn't want him thinking of her as helpless, either. "You don't have to."

"I didn't say I had to. I asked if you wanted me to," he pointed out.

On the other hand, she didn't want to come off like someone who slapped away a helping hand, either.

"Yes, please. That would be very nice of you," she told him.

Chance was out the door before the last word had left her lips. He was back just as quickly, juggling both suitcases as well as the three boxes. It amazed her that he hadn't dropped anything.

"You certainly move fast," she marveled.

"It's a little something you pick up when people are shooting at you," he told her. Looking around the room for a likely spot, he asked, "Where do you want me to put these?"

"Doesn't matter, just any place," she said vaguely. "I've got to empty the suitcases and hang the things up inside that shallow closet." She waved at the small door that was off to one side.

He set the suitcases and boxes down next to the sofa. "Again, that wouldn't be a problem for me—if I had a closet," he added with a hint of a grin.

"You don't have a closet?" Chloe asked, surprised, trying to visualize his living quarters.

"Does a footlocker count?"

"Only if you're in boot camp," she said before she realized that he was being serious.

Chance grinned at the reference. It hit home. "Well, it's kind of like that," he told her.

Picking up one of the suitcases, Chloe placed it on the sofa and snapped opened the locks, then lifted the lid.

Chance caught himself looking into the suitcase. Instead of the jeans and practical shirts he'd expected, he saw that she had packed several very flowery, pastel-colored dresses. The kind, he thought, that seemed more suited to sitting on a porch swing, sipping lemonade, than following around teenage boys as they did their chores on a ranch. From what Graham had explained, Peter's Place had been founded on the idea that the chores were what taught these troubled kids discipline and doing those chores in turn brought order to their lives.

Somehow, that kind of dusty activity just didn't seem compatible with flowing, feminine dresses. At least not to him.

She saw Chance looking rather skeptically at what she'd packed. She could almost read his thoughts by the expression on his face.

He was probably right, she thought. What she'd brought with her wasn't all that sensible. It reflected who and what she was, but it fell short in the practicality department.

Still, as long as Chance didn't bring the subject up, she wasn't about to try to defend her choices.

She thought of something that Chance had said when he brought her suitcases in. Something that had made her think of Donnie. She'd understood her husband's reasons for joining up, just like she understood what Chance had said about it the other day. Fighting for your country were sentiments to be admired. But they were also idealistic and they didn't explain how Chance had dealt with the day-to-day struggle of just trying to survive.

"How did you stand it?" she asked Chance suddenly.

He looked at her, confused. She had him at a complete disadvantage. The question had come out of the blue, and since they weren't actually talking about anything, he really wasn't sure what Chloe was referring to.

"How did I stand what?" he wanted to know.

"When you brought the boxes and suitcases in, you said you learned to move fast because people were

shooting at you. How did you stand that?" she asked
in all sincerity. "Knowing that any second, no matter
what you were doing and how quiet it was, someone
could just start shooting at you? Worse, that they might
actually wind up killing you?"

"Most of the time I didn't think about it," he told her
honestly. "You really can't spend time thinking about
it, or it'll wind up paralyzing you. You just hope that
when someone does start shooting at you, the bullet
won't have your name on it. Or that you get to return
fire quickly enough and accurately enough to take out
whoever it is who wants you dead." He paused, his eyes
meeting hers. "Everyone who goes over there just wants
to get home in one piece."

Chance watched as Chloe slowly unpacked, neatly
hanging up the dresses. He could easily envision her
wearing those dresses, a soft spring breeze flirting with
the material, causing it to lightly press against her body
in ways that could make a grown man weak.

He felt his stomach muscles tightening and forced
himself to breathe.

He had no business thinking like that about her,
Chance told himself.

Just like he had no business asking her questions,
yet here he was, doing both.

He had to watch that, Chance upbraided himself.

Even so, he heard himself telling her, "You know,
whenever you're ready to talk about it, I'm here to listen."

"'Talk about it'?" she asked quizzically. Was Chance
just talking in general, or was he somehow intuitively

referring to the single loss that had ultimately broken her heart?

Chance felt as if he was getting in too deep, but now that he had opened the door, he had no choice except to continue.

"Talk about whoever it is that you lost," he explained. "I figure it has to be someone in the military. Even with all the communication we have available today, it still has to be tough, being cut off like that. Not knowing what's going on until a lot later—if at all."

He knew he wasn't great with words, but he did have a sense of empathy and he knew without putting it into words what she had to have felt. What she still might be feeling. Because he had gone through the same thing.

"Thank you," Chloe said quietly.

She sounded sincere. Awkward or not, maybe he'd pushed the right buttons after all.

"Then you do want to talk?" he asked.

"No." She'd actually thanked him for the offer, not for the opportunity. "No offense, but I can't. Not yet."

Maybe not ever, she added silently because she didn't know if she actually could. The mere thought hurt too much.

"But if and when I am ready to talk about 'it,'" she said, deliberately using his terminology, "I'll take you up on that offer."

Chance nodded. "Good enough," he told her. "I'll be around." He realized how that had to have sounded, so he amended the last sentence. "At least for now."

That last comment caught Chloe off guard. "You make it sound temporary. Is there a time limit to the job?" she asked, wondering if there was something Graham had said to Chance before they had come out of his den yesterday after the interview.

Chance answered her honestly. "Only the one I set for myself," he said. "I only stay in any one place for as long as it feels right. When it stops feeling right, that's when it's time to go."

That sounded just too nomadic for her. If things were working out, why would he want to leave? It didn't make sense.

"And what makes it time to go?" she challenged.

No one had ever questioned his actions before. But Chloe put him on the spot. Though it made him uneasy, it also had him looking at her in a different light. The woman had spunk, he had to admit.

He shrugged. "Just a feeling. Can't really put it into better words than that," he confessed.

Chloe assessed his words. Was he running from something without realizing it? she couldn't help wondering.

"Maybe that feeling is fear," she suggested. She saw that her suggestion did not please him. But she honestly believed what she was saying to him. She couldn't apologize for that; it would be a lie. Instead, she tried to explain what she meant. "Maybe what you fear is complacency. You get too comfortable, too used to something, and you start to worry that you're losing your edge, that you're getting soft. That the challenge is gone. So you have to leave to find another mountain to climb, another dragon to slay."

Chance looked at her as if she was suddenly babbling nonsense.

"I'm not climbing any mountains, and I sure as hell am not slaying any of those dragons. Anyway, dragons aren't real." He was trying his best not to sound annoyed—but he was.

"No," she agreed, "they're not."

He knew he should just go. Normally, he would have. But something was making him dig in his heels and stay. He wanted to get something straight.

"Is this the kind of stuff you're going to be feeding those boys?" he asked. "Stuff about slaying dragons?"

"No, this is the kind of 'stuff' I'm going to be using in order to try to understand the boys," she said. "To help them reconnect with the world."

He laughed drily. Still sounded like a bunch of mumbo jumbo to him.

"Well, good luck with that," he told her, shaking his head. "But if you ask me, a little hard work and a little responsibility should help those boys do all the reconnecting that they need."

"Hard work and responsibility," she repeated as if he had just quoted scripture. "Has it helped you?" Chloe asked innocently.

His scowl deepened for a moment, and then he just waved her words away. "Don't try getting inside my head, Chloe Elliott. There's nothing in it for you. I'm doing just fine just the way I am."

She suppressed a sigh. "Okay, as long as you're happy."

Happy? When was the last time he'd been happy? He couldn't remember.

"Happy's got nothing to do with it," Chance answered. "I'm my own man on my own terms, and that's all that really counts."

He felt himself losing his temper, and he didn't want to do that. Once things were said, they couldn't get "unsaid" and a lot of damage could be done. He didn't want that to happen. Not with this woman.

"I'd better go find the boss. Graham said that he wanted to take me around the spread as soon as I stashed my gear."

She didn't want to be the reason he was late. "Then I guess you'd better get going."

"Yeah, I guess I'd better." With that, he crossed back to the door.

He walked out feeling that there were things left unspoken. A great many things. But then, maybe it was better that way. He wasn't looking to have his head "shrunk" any more than it already was. Even if the lady doing the shrinking was nothing short of a knockout.

Some things, he reasoned, were just better off left alone.

Chapter Six

Chloe could feel the butterflies in her stomach. Flexing, but at present unable to fly. They were huge butterflies with wingspans that would make an eagle seriously jealous.

But as she walked to her first meeting with the boys at Peter's Place, she knew that if she gave any indication that she was even slightly nervous—never mind that she was about a minute away from having a full-on panic attack—she was certain to lose any advantage and all credibility. Putting up a calm front was all-important during this first encounter.

She was well aware that this would set the tone for the rest of the visits to come.

No pressure here, Chloe mocked herself.

But she knew that if she didn't project that she was

completely in control of the situation, word would spread to the other boys immediately, and then none of them would view her with the respect she needed in order to be of any help to them.

And helping them was why she was here, why she'd become a counselor in the first place.

And maybe, in helping others to heal, eventually she'd find a way to help and heal herself.

When she took the job, she'd assumed that she would be conducting a group session, with Sasha present, in which she'd get to meet all four of the boys at once and learn a little about each of them by the time the session was over.

But Sasha had been concerned that since this was her maiden run, so to speak, she might be a little overwhelmed meeting four teens at once. Graham's wife had suggested that she start out small, talking just to one of the ranch residents at a time.

Naturally, Chloe had agreed. She thought that a one-on-one meeting might work a little more in her favor. Besides, she didn't have a ton of experience. New on the job, she needed to abide by Sasha's wishes. After all, Sasha was the expert here.

So here she was, walking into the small, cheery room that had been set aside in the main house for counseling sessions, doing her best to try to control the squadron of butterflies in her stomach that were morphing into Boeing 747s.

At least the sun was cooperating, she noted, filling the room with warm light thanks to the full-length windows that looked out onto the corral and the stables beyond that.

The sun might be cooperating, but her first patient didn't look as if he was inclined to follow suit.

Brandon Baker eyed her suspiciously the moment he walked into the room less than a couple of seconds after she'd entered. A good-looking fifteen-year-old with dark, almost black hair and brown eyes, he was a lot thinner than he should have been. His stance and his very gait exuded defiance.

His eyes quickly swept around the room. "Where's the doc?" he wanted to know.

Chloe didn't bother asking him if he meant Sasha. That would be stalling. "She won't be joining us for the session," Chloe began.

Brandon made a 180 without missing a step and headed for the doorway he'd just entered through.

Chloe knew she had to say something quickly or he'd be gone in a flash. She called after him. "Mrs. Fortune Robinson thought we could get to know each other better if she wasn't here."

Brandon had his hand on the doorknob and didn't bother turning around. "She thought wrong," he said flatly.

"Come back and sit down, Brandon."

Chloe hadn't raised her voice and she definitely wasn't shouting, but there was no mistaking the firmness in her tone. It wasn't a request; it was an order. She surprised even herself.

Brandon still didn't turn around, but neither did he

turn the doorknob and go out. It was as if he was still waiting to be convinced.

"Now, please," she requested.

Brandon blew out a breath, turned around and then walked over to the folding chair that was set up opposite hers.

Chloe gestured toward the padded green chair. "Sit, please." Both words were given equal weight.

After a moment, during which time she had a feeling the boy was mentally going over his options, as well as wondering how far he could push her, Brandon Baker finally sat down.

"Okay, I'm sitting." He looked at her, but she couldn't read the expression on his face. All she knew was that it wasn't warm. "Now what?"

"Now we talk," Chloe told him in as bright and engaging a tone as she could summon.

"Talk?" The single word seemed to mock her, and she saw a smirk on Brandon's sullen face. "Lady, I don't even know you."

"That's where the talking part comes in," she told him in as upbeat a manner as she could project. "We talk so that we can get to know each other."

"And then what?" he challenged cynically. "Become best friends?"

"Maybe," she allowed. "Eventually. If enough time passes."

The scowl on the young face was dark and forbidding. "I don't need any more friends."

"Maybe not," Chloe said agreeably. "Maybe you're one of those people who have all the friends he needs—

although I doubt it," she couldn't help adding. A warning look rose in Brandon's eyes. Chloe pushed on. "But it's obvious that you do need a way to get rid of all that anger you're holding on to."

Brandon shifted restlessly, indicating that he had heard all that he was willing to listen to. His eyes narrowed. "Look, lady—"

"Chloe," she supplied. She knew that she should have told the boy to address her by either her surname or simply "ma'am," but somehow, using her first name just seemed friendlier and she needed to find some sort of an opening if she was going to forge a bridge between them.

Brandon looked bored. "Whatever," he said dismissively. And then, in case there were any lingering doubts about the situation, he told her in no uncertain terms, "I don't know what you thought when you came here, but I'm not some kind of a guinea pig for you to practice on so you can earn your merit badge or whatever it is you're trying to get out of this."

She realized that he was trying to get her angry, angry enough to walk out. She had no intentions of letting him.

"What I'm trying to 'get out of this' is to find a way to help you help yourself," she explained patiently. "No matter how you feel about it, Brandon, I'm not the enemy here."

"Okay, you're not the enemy," he parroted. "*Now* can I go?" he demanded.

Chloe glanced at her watch—as if she wasn't keenly

aware of every second that went by. "We've got another forty-five minutes left to the session."

Brandon slouched in his chair, crossing his arms defiantly across his chest as he glared at her. "So you're what, a shrink?" he wanted to know, his hostility almost palpable.

"I'm a counselor," she corrected, fervently wishing she had more ammunition at her disposal for this battle she suddenly found herself in.

"Uh-huh." Hostility momentarily turned to boredom, and he deliberately yawned. "Same difference."

"Not exactly," she told him. In actuality, there was a world of difference, especially in the two disciplines' approaches to the people they dealt with. But she wasn't about to bore Brandon further by explaining them. "Tell you what," she said instead, "why don't I ask you some questions and you can fill in the blanks for me. How would that be?"

He made no answer, other than to scowl and to slouch even lower in his chair, his body language telling her that he didn't care one way or another what she proposed to do.

Chloe had to concentrate not to allow the hand that was holding Brandon's file to tremble. Showing fear was the worst thing she could do, and she knew it.

"According to the information on your entrance form, you had an older brother, Blake, who was killed—"

Brandon instantly sat up, and his body became almost rigid as his eyes blazed accusingly at her. "You shut up about my brother!" he ordered.

She couldn't do that. If she hadn't thought so before,

she knew now that Blake was at the root of Brandon's anger. Chloe pressed on.

She understood what he was going through better than he knew, she thought.

"Your brother did a noble thing," she told him in a calm, even voice. "Don't you think that should be acknowledged?"

"No!" Brandon shouted at her. And then he cried, "My brother did a stupid thing! If he hadn't joined the military, he wouldn't have gotten himself killed. He'd still be alive today. He'd still be here! With me!" His voice cracked as he made the declaration.

"Brandon," Chloe continued in a quiet voice, doing her best to try to calm him, "I know that you're hurting right now—"

His temper flared again. "Don't talk like you know me!" He jumped to his feet now. "You don't know anything about me!" he insisted furiously.

Chloe refused to back down. If she retreated right now, she might as well give up. "I might not know you, but I know how you feel," she told him doggedly as she tried again.

"No, you don't! Don't say that!" The boy looked like he was fighting back tears. "Nobody knows how I feel!"

With that, Brandon dashed right past her and out the door.

He would have dashed down the hall and presumably out of the house if he hadn't run straight into Chance, blindly colliding with the towering cowboy.

The impact might have knocked Brandon to the floor

if Chance hadn't reacted quickly and caught hold of the boy by his shoulders.

"Hey, where's the fire?" Chance asked. The next moment, he saw Chloe coming up behind the fleeing boy. He saw the look of concern on her face. "Everything all right here?" he wanted to know.

Unlike his first question, this one was addressed to Chloe.

"Everything's all right," she told Chance resolutely. She caught the surprised look that Brandon slanted her way. "I just decided to end the session a little earlier than planned. Since this is our first session, I thought maybe Brandon needed a little time to digest what we talked about before we could move forward."

Chance looked at the boy he was still holding steady. He had his doubts about the validity of what Chloe was telling him.

"Is that so?" he asked, looking at the boy.

Brandon shot a look toward Chloe, and Chance could read his thoughts. The teen was calculating his next move, deciding if now was the time to play the odds or to just go along with things.

His gaze flickered as if he'd decided to run with the excuse Chloe had handed him. "Yeah, getting used to someone new takes time. The doc's giving me time."

Chance looked over the boy's head at Chloe. "Is that what you're doing, Doc?" he asked, even though he was highly skeptical about the excuse he was being given. "Are you giving Brandon time so he can get used to you?"

Chloe nodded. "This was an introductory session

only," she said, her eyes meeting Brandon's. "The next one will be longer. Right, Brandon?"

Rather than agree, Brandon merely raised and lowered his thin shoulders in a careless, disinterested shrug. "You're the doc," the boy replied.

"Well, since you're free," Chance told the boy, "there's that stall waiting for you to muck out." He saw the face that Brandon unintentionally made. He didn't pretend not to notice. "You know the rules. Chores first, then you can ride—unless of course you want to talk to the doc here some more," Chance said, offering the boy a choice.

Brandon waited, as if he was actually weighing his options for a second. And then he made his choice. "I'll be at the stable."

He walked toward the rear of the ranch house to the exit closest to the stable.

Chance turned his attention to Chloe and saw the disappointed expression on her face. "Didn't go all that well, huh?"

He was kidding, right? "Well, I just took second place to cleaning out manure in a horse stall, so no, it didn't go all that well."

Chance laughed, not at her but at the situation. "Don't take it personally. The kid's mad at the world right now." Graham had given him a quick background summary for all four of the boys. Chance felt for them, even if he wasn't prone to showing it. "He looked up to his big brother, thought of him as invincible. When it turned out that his brother wasn't bulletproof, it threw the kid for a loop. He's still trying to find a place for himself in a world that no longer has his big brother in it. That is *not* an easy adjustment to make," he told her. "Especially at Brandon's age."

"Losing someone is not an easy adjustment to make at *any* age," she told Chance in no uncertain terms. "I was trying to tell Brandon that. Trying to let him know that I understand what he's going through."

Chance was closer to the boy's situation than he cared to admit, so he tried to explain to her just what she was up against.

"He's not ready to hear that," Chance told her. "Right now, he's wrapping himself up in that pain and anger that he feels. That rage. It's the only way he has to cope. Without it, he's afraid that he'll just break down, fall to pieces and never be able to get back up. Being angry is all he has," Chance stressed, trying to make her understand. "You take that away from the boy before he's ready to let it go and, well, there's no telling what can happen."

It was a warning. He didn't want her good heart to accidentally cause her to make a really bad mistake. He had a feeling that she'd never forgive herself.

Chloe laughed shortly. He had a better handle on the situation than she did, she thought ruefully. "You know, you sound pretty wise for a cowboy."

The corners of Chance's full mouth curved just the slightest bit. "I think, on behalf of cowboys everywhere, I should be taking offense at that."

She wasn't getting anything right today, was she? "I didn't mean it that way," she told him apologetically.

He laughed and stopped her before she could launch

into a full-scale apology. He'd just been trying to tease her out of her very serious mood. "I know. I'm just having fun with you."

It was her turn to turn the tables on him. "You can do that?" she asked, pretending to be surprised. "You can have fun?"

"I've been known to," Chance deadpanned. "Every once in a while."

It suddenly occurred to her that Chance was standing much too close to her. So close, she wondered if he could hear her heart beating fast. So close that she was sure he could easily kiss her without any effort at all.

And although the thought of being kissed by Chance did instantly raise her pulse rate, Chloe knew that kissing him would be a huge mistake, especially for her. Because being kissed by and kissing Chance would mean opening a door to a place she had absolutely no desire to revisit.

A place filled with feelings.

The very idea of having feelings for someone—*those* kinds of feelings—much less falling in love with that person, scared Chloe beyond words.

And right now, she needed all her words in order to reach the four boys whose care she had been charged with. That left her no time for anything else, she silently lectured herself. No racing pulses, no pounding hearts. No sexy cowboy to cause her imagination to take flight.

"Um, I'd better get ready for my next session," she told Chance, backing away.

"Who are you seeing?" he asked.

Good. She could talk about work. There was safety

in that. "Will Sherman. Hopefully, I'll do better my first time out with him than I did with Brandon."

He'd asked her who she was seeing next for a reason. So he could offer her some help. It was obvious that she needed it.

"That one's got trust issues," he told her. "Because his mother turned on him and beat him so badly, he's closed down. But the good news is that he really doesn't want to be like that. You can make a connection if you're patient enough. Just go slow, and listen. He'll open up eventually."

"Sounds like he already has," Chloe said. "With you."

Chance didn't want her thinking that he was treading on her toes. "No, I'm just good at reading signs," he told her. And then, in an effort to make her understand, he reminded her, "I'm good with horses." It wasn't a boast, just a fact. "They don't talk, either. But if you watch them closely, you get to understand what they want, what they need. Once you know that, gaining their trust is easy and inevitable. Same goes for people, too."

She smiled at him. He'd just summarized an entire year's worth of studies in a few sentences. The man was a natural, she thought. He should probably be in her place.

But there was no sense in talking herself out of a job she both wanted and needed, Chloe thought. So she simply said, "Thank you. I'll keep that in mind. Now I'd better get ready for my next session."

He nodded. "And that's my cue to get out of here," he said—just before he did.

Chapter Seven

The 747s in her stomach were finally down to the manageable size of normal butterflies. Maybe even *small* butterflies, Chloe thought.

She'd been counseling the boys for a couple of weeks now and she was slowly getting used to it, to the routine that Sasha had instituted. After enduring rather tense initial sessions with each of the four boys, she knew what she was up against with them now. They were coming to the office for private sessions three, sometimes four times a week. More if any of them felt they needed it or if they sought a little extra guidance with something they were attempting to work out.

Although conducting a one-on-one had been admittedly scary to her at first, Chloe decided that maybe Sasha was right after all. The four boys had plenty of time to interact with one another while they did their chores and when they spent time riding under Chance's supervision, not to mention that they were always all together at mealtime.

Going with the philosophy that everyone needed their own space and the idea that the boys might be more inclined to open up about something that was bothering them if they didn't have to make a public declaration of it, Chloe continued to see each of them on an individual basis rather than meeting with them as a group.

The two boys who had been at Peter's Place longer were in a better place mentally than the two newer arrivals. Jonah and Ryan had had more time to work out their anger and the issues that had brought them here in the first place. Happily, they both seemed as if they had gotten back on track again after their emotional derailments had threatened to turn them into repeat offenders. Thanks in part to her and to Sasha's joint efforts, both boys were learning how to cope with the curves that life had thrown at them and might very well throw at them again.

None of the battles had been won yet, especially not in the individual cases of Brandon and Will, but Chloe felt that the latter two were definitely taking baby steps in the right direction. It made her proud that she could say that she was a part of their progress, slow though it might seem.

Her own life might still need some work, Chloe thought, but at least she was helping four teens with their whole lives ahead of them work toward fulfilling their destinies. That was definitely something to be proud of, she told herself.

"You look pretty happy with yourself," Chance observed the next time that their paths crossed—which unbeknownst to her was as often as Chance could make happen. Ordinarily, he would have kept to himself the way he usually did, but there was something about this woman that just seemed to burrow into him, to pull him out of the solitary state he'd learned to prefer. She made him remember another time when life hadn't been so deadly serious. When sadness hadn't been his constant companion.

"Actually, I am—kind of," she added, lest Chance think she had an ego problem, or that she was giving herself way too much credit.

Chance read between the lines. "I take it that things are going well on your end with the boys," he guessed. He leaned against the doorjamb to her office. "I don't hear any of them grumbling in the corral anymore. Oh, Brandon still has a bit of an attitude problem when it comes to doing some of his chores, but even he's toned down somewhat in the last week. So I guess whatever it is you're doing here with them, you're doing it right," he told her with an encouraging grin. Then he summed it up simply. "It's working."

He was being kind, she thought. This wasn't just her doing. She really doubted that the tall, quiet cowboy was unaware of the effect that he had on the boys.

"Thanks, but I realize that it's a team effort. What you do with them when they're with you is just as important when it comes to stabilizing their mental health and turning them into well-adjusted young men as what's being said here in this room when the door's closed."

Chloe couldn't help thinking that Chance was the epitome of the strong silent type, enduring things without complaint, and that had to make a real impression on these boys, all of whom were in need of a strong father figure they could look up to and use as a role model. Even if they didn't consciously realize it.

Chance merely nodded, not about to argue with her about it. Arguing had always seemed like a waste of time to him.

"If you say so. Say, are you free now?" he asked suddenly. "I don't know what Sasha's got you doing when you're not counseling the boys, but I'm going to have them out in the corral, exercising their horses in a few minutes, and you're welcomed to come out and watch. Maybe it'll help you with their sessions later on," he speculated. Then a rather infectious smile split his lips. "Who knows, you might even enjoy getting a little fresh air. It might get to be habit-forming," Chance teased.

"Are you hinting that I'm some kind of a hermit?" Chloe retorted. Was that how he saw her? The idea bothered her more than she was willing to admit.

Chance looked perfectly serious as he elaborated. "Not a hermit, exactly. Hermits don't interact with people. But what are those people called? You know the ones I mean," he said, as if hunting for the correct word. "The ones who don't go out in daylight?"

Her eyebrows rose up so high that they all but disappeared beneath her bangs. "Vampires?" she guessed, stunned. "Are you saying I'm a vampire?"

"Well, no, not exactly," he said, backtracking just a little. "You definitely don't suck blood or anything like that, but those vampires you mentioned, they're supposed to have a thing about not going out into the daylight, don't they?"

"I wouldn't know," she informed him a little stiffly.

"Well, I've heard talk," Chance allowed, completely deadpan. But then a smile teased the corners of his mouth, bringing out the same sexy dimples in his cheeks, the ones that made her stare at him, dream about him, even though she told herself not to. "I'm just messing with you," he admitted with a laugh that backed up his words. "But you are kind of pale," he pointed out a little more seriously.

Chloe wanted to protest, but in good conscience, she couldn't. She knew she really was pale, especially in comparison with Chance.

So instead, she inclined her head, conceding the point. "I guess I do stay indoors a lot."

"Well, there's one way to fix that," Chance said, reminding her of the invitation he'd just extended to her a couple of minutes ago. "Come outside to the corral and watch the boys put their horses through their paces. You might even find that you enjoy it. I kind of suspect that the boys will enjoy showing you what they've learned when it comes to handling horses, seeing as all of them were city kids when they came here."

Initially, she'd thought of Chance as being exceptionally closed-mouthed. She was going to have to reassess her original impression of the man.

"You know, for a man who claims not to be much of a talker, you certainly do know how to sell something," she told him with genuine admiration.

He looked at her in all innocence, as if he had no idea what she was talking about.

"I'm not selling anything," he told her. "I'm just telling you the way things are. Nothing more, nothing less. If you're interested in *really* joining in," he went on, "we've got a real gentle mare in the stable named Mirabel. Mirabel wouldn't hurt a fly. You can saddle her up and ride her along with the boys if you want."

Chloe was already vigorously shaking her head. "No, that's okay. No riding. I'll come out to watch the boys, but I'm just coming along as a spectator, not as a rider," she told Chance emphatically.

She'd succeeded in arousing his curiosity. "You ever been on a horse?"

"This is Texas," Chloe told him, as if that fact should be enough of an answer for him.

But he saw what she was trying to do. Chloe was being evasive, trying to use a diversion rather than answering his question outright.

Chance smiled at her. "I know where we are. I didn't ask you that. I asked if you've ever been on a horse. A moving horse," he specified in case she was going to pretend that she thought he meant a merry-go-round or a hobby horse of some sort.

Chloe bristled for a moment. She didn't like being cornered. She also didn't like admitting to any shortcomings, and as she'd already said, this *was* Texas, where everyone was thought to be born on the back of a horse, or at least knowing how to ride one.

For a second, she thought of bluffing her way through this, but then she decided that he was undoubtedly going to find out sooner or later. Better to tell Chance the truth, embarrassing though she felt it was, than be caught in a lie, which, when she came right down to it, was even more embarrassing to her.

"My whole childhood was a hand-to-mouth existence for my late mother and me. Horseback riding was a luxury we couldn't afford—or even have time for, actually," Chloe told him honestly, a solemn look on her face. "I grew up in a run-down section of the city. There was no 'horse next door,'" she quipped.

Chance nodded, straightening. His relaxed stance was gone as his eyes met hers and he looked at her intently. For a moment, she couldn't read his expression.

"So then you don't know how to ride a horse," he concluded.

"I thought that was what I was telling you," she said with a touch of impatience.

He nodded, as if he had just been given a problem to work with. Taking her elbow as he spoke, he carefully urged her toward the doorway, and then guided her out. "We're going to have to take care of that little oversight first chance we get."

The last thing she wanted was to have him see her being inept at something. "I think we both have a lot more pressing things to concern ourselves with than my lack of riding skills," she told him. They were being paid to work with the boys, not to broaden their own skills.

"No law that says we can't do more than just one thing," he replied. Long ago, Chance had learned when to retreat, so for now, he did. "For starters, just come with me to watch the boys. You'll see there's nothing to be afraid of." The easy smile was back as Chance told her, "Think of it as getting two birds with one stone."

She was keenly aware that he'd used the word *afraid*. Was that what he thought? That she was afraid of horses? Afraid of riding?

"I'm not afraid of riding a horse," she protested. "I told you, it's just something I never got around to."

"If you're not afraid, that's good," he pronounced. "That's one less thing for you to overcome."

She'd been so focused on what he was saying—and on trying to dispel this afraid-of-her-own-shadow image he seemed to have of her—that she didn't realize he had brought her out behind the back of the house. They'd gone past the guesthouse, where she was staying, and over to the corral.

All four boys were already there, along with the horses whose grooming and feeding they were each charged with. Five horses were saddled and ready to be ridden, even though the boys still had their feet firmly planted on the ground.

Jonah, who'd been there the longest and in everyone's estimation had come along the furthest, was standing between two horses, the one he had been caring for the last few months and the one that Chance rode when he was out riding with them.

Chance nodded at Jonah in acknowledgment, but before taking his stallion's reins from him, he turned toward Chloe first.

"You'll be all right here?"

She was surprised that he took the time to take her into consideration. "You asking me or telling me?" She couldn't tell from his tone.

That small smile she was growing so familiar with curved just the corners of his mouth. "Asking, mostly," he replied.

She didn't see why he was concerned. For the most part, she was out of the way here. "Sure—unless you suddenly decide to all ride toward me, at which point I'll probably be flattened."

Chance suppressed a wider smile as he shook his head. "Nope, no flattening. Not on the agenda today," he told her. And then he nodded toward the fence directly behind her. "If you want, you can climb up on the fence and straddle it. You'll get a better view that way," he told her.

Chloe looked over her shoulder, glancing at the fence a little uncertainly, even though she told him, "Maybe I will."

He caught the hesitancy and recognized it for what it was. Chloe wasn't one for climbing, he guessed. "Need a boost?" he asked.

Just because he asked, she was determined not to accept it. She tossed her head, sending her blond hair flying over her shoulders. "No, I can manage," she informed him.

But she actually couldn't, she discovered as she attempted to climb up the fence's slats.

Just as she realized she was in serious danger of falling backward and not just embarrassing herself but possibly hurting herself as well, she felt a very firm hand on her backside.

Sucking in her breath, she tried to look over her shoulder only to have Chance chide, "Steady or you're liable to fall. I'm not getting fresh here, I'm just trying to keep you from breaking anything fairly important," he told her. And then the next second, as he helped get her to the top, he declared with a note of triumph, "There you go. Now you've got a better view. Just don't get it into your head to leave before I get back to help you down," he warned.

And with that, Chance headed over to the cluster of boys.

He nodded at Jonah. "Thank you," he said as he took the reins from the group's oldest member. "Looks like we've got ourselves an audience today, boys. Show her what you've learned—and remember, don't embarrass me or yourselves," he reminded them as if that was one of the rules of procedure instead of something he was just now telling them.

"Is she going to be riding with us?" Ryan wanted to know.

"No, Ms. Elliott's strictly here as an observer," Chance answered. "So, no fancy stuff—and no slacking off, either," he told the boys. "Just nice and easy, like I showed you." He glanced toward Brandon, who looked as if he was ready to kick the horse's flanks and lead the others in a gallop around the corral. "Nice and easy, Brandon," he repeated with emphasis. "This isn't the preliminary trial for the Kentucky Derby. Remember, these are horses, not your personal toys," he warned them. "You push your horse too hard and you're back on stable duty—full-time. Are we clear?" he asked, looking around at the four faces before him.

"Clear," they all responded, their young voices blending together.

Chance nodded. "Okay then, let's show Ms. Elliott what you've learned."

Delighted, Chloe watched as the boys put the horses through their paces. The gaits varied from simply walking along the perimeter of the corral, to trotting to finally galloping at a moderate pace. She thought that was the end of it, but then she saw that the boys began leading their horses through several other exercises, one of which involved weaving in and out as if they were following the beat of a song that only they could hear.

When they were finally finished, the four riders lined up next to each other and then, almost in unison, turned toward her to see if she had enjoyed the show they had put on for her.

Chloe applauded enthusiastically. "That's wonderful," she told the boys.

"I wouldn't exactly say *wonderful*," Chance told her, bringing his own horse up to where she was perched on the fence. "But at least they've learned to follow the rules." He paused, looking at the four boys, who brought their mounts closer to where Chloe was sitting. "I'm talking about the boys, not the horses. The horses already knew how to follow the rules. All they needed was to have someone issue them."

Turning in his saddle, he looked at her. "So, how about it?"

His question came out of the blue and caught her completely off guard. "How about what?"

"Are you willing to give it a try now?" Chance wanted to know.

She suddenly realized that there were five sets of eyes turned in her direction, waiting for her to answer.

Chapter Eight

It took Chloe a minute before she realized that the cowboy was serious. When she did, she was quick to respond to his question.

"No, not right now," she told Chance, doing her best to avoid looking at the four boys. "I've got all that paperwork I need to catch up on," she added vaguely, coming up with the first excuse she could think of.

With care and effort, she managed to climb down off the fence.

But she found that her exit was blocked, not just by Chance, but by the boys, still on their horses, as well.

"C'mon, Ms. Elliott. Try it. It'll be fun," Ryan coaxed.

"We won't let anything happen to you," Jonah promised solemnly, adding his voice to the others. "Mirabel really *is* the gentlest horse on the ranch, honest."

"And Jonah and I will ride on either side of you, to make sure you don't fall off," Ryan added, obviously thinking she needed extra convincing.

It was clear that they thought she was inept when it came to horses, never mind that she really was. She didn't want that shortcoming to be general knowledge. That was the sort of thing that would make her stick out like a sore thumb on the ranch.

She looked accusingly at Chance. "What did you tell them?"

"Not a thing," Chance answered. "They're capable of figuring things out on their own."

"Horses aren't anything to be afraid of," Brandon told her, speaking up. Then he glanced at his bunk-mate. "Right, Will?"

The latter flushed. When he opened his mouth, it became apparent why. "Hey, when I came here, I'd never been around a horse before." He gestured to the mount he was on. "But I learned how to ride."

"You rode very well," Chloe told him, impressed. She was well aware of the fact that it had taken a lot of work for the boys to be able to ride as effortlessly as they did now. "You all did," she added. And then Chloe looked around at all four of their faces. The light dawned on her. "Oh, I see what you're doing."

The face Ryan turned toward her was one of complete innocence. "What are we doing?"

Like he didn't know. "You're trying to get me so caught up in what you're telling me that I forget all about not wanting to get up on a horse and riding it.

That horse," she amended, seeing the saddled dapple gray mare that Chance was leading toward her.

"Will you?" Jonah asked.

"We meant what we said. Jonah and I won't let Mirabel run off with you—not that she ever would," Ryan quickly added. "I'm just saying what you're thinking."

"So now I've turned you all into mind readers, huh? I guess the sessions are going better than I thought they were," she told the boys with a grin. She was feeling rather proud of her accomplishments when it came to the teens. Which just reinforced her determination not to look like an inept fool around them.

"Now *you're* doing it," Ryan told her, shooting her a shrewd look.

She looked at him innocently. "Doing what?"

"You're trying to distract us," Ryan told her. "You're getting us to talk about something else so we forget about giving you that riding lesson."

It was like being faced with four tenacious pit bulls. Once they sank their teeth into her, they were holding on for dear life. Well, she could play that game, as well. "I don't need a riding lesson," she protested.

Chance brought his horse closer to her. "I thought those sessions of yours were all about always telling the truth," he said.

They were really ganging up on her, she thought. But she was determined to stand her ground. "They are."

"Well?" he asked, looking at her pointedly. She didn't have to look at the boys; she felt their stares. They were all thinking the same thing, that she wasn't owning up to her shortcoming.

And then it occurred to her how to answer them. "I don't need a riding lesson because I don't *want* to know how to ride. Now if you boys—" she deliberately looked at all of them, including Chance "—will excuse me, I really do have work to do. But good job, all of you," she told them again enthusiastically.

With that, Chloe made her way back to the main house, keenly aware that she was being watched by five sets of eyes as she walked.

She really did have work to catch up on, she thought defensively. It just wasn't as pressing as she made it sound.

What *was* pressing was her need to get away. *Now.*

Chloe wasn't sure if she imagined the knock on her door that evening until she heard it a second time. There was definitely someone at her door.

It was after dinner and rather than linger at the big house with Graham and his family the way she had done on several occasions now, Chloe had left the table early and retreated to her quarters in the guesthouse. She wanted a little time to herself to regroup.

She was still feeling somewhat uncomfortable about this afternoon and the fact that she'd had trouble owning up to not being able to ride.

She had to remember that it was okay not to be perfect, she told herself. It was just that she was trying really hard to present a strong front before these boys.

Maybe, she thought, it was one of them at the door. Perhaps one of them wanted to talk to her about this afternoon. Probably to give her more of a pep talk, she surmised.

Chloe smiled to herself. They were all rather sweet in their own way, and she appreciated that they were trying to be supportive of her.

Maybe she'd just forget about being nervous and throw herself into learning how to ride. It seemed like practically everyone in the state did it, she reasoned. How hard could it be?

It was definitely something to think about.

Tomorrow.

Psyching herself up, Chloe swung open the door. The cheery "Hi" she was about to utter never made an appearance when she saw it wasn't any of the boys standing on her doorstep.

It was Chance.

Ever since she'd lost Donnie, her first thoughts always seemed to entertain a dark explanation. "Is something wrong?" Chloe asked, her heart already lodged in her throat.

Chance's answer was annoyingly vague. "That depends on your point of view."

Damn it, for a plainspoken man he could be maddeningly unclear. "Meaning?" she demanded.

He crossed the threshold, but made no effort to come any farther into her quarters than that. "Meaning that you tried to lie to those boys."

He was referring to her initial pretense of knowing how to ride. She didn't care for his accusation, especially in light of the way things turned out. "Well, they wound up hearing the truth so it's not really lying, is it?"

His eyes pinned hers, making her want to squirm. "What would you call it?"

She could tell him exactly what she would call it. "I'd call it not wanting them to think any less of me."

That didn't make any sense to Chance. "Because you can't ride?" he asked incredulously. Why would they think any less of her for that? "Why? You never told them you traveled with the rodeo as a trick rider."

Why did she think he would understand her motivation? The cowboy had probably never known an insecure moment in his life. He was perfect at everything he did, and he knew it.

"Let's just drop it, all right?" she said shortly.

"Sure," he agreed, then added one condition. "As soon as you come out with me." Just to ensure that she would, Chance caught her hand in his and began to lead her outside.

Not wanting to cause a scene, she went along reluctantly. "Just where are we going?" she wanted to know.

"Don't look so spooked," he said with a short laugh. "I'm not kidnapping you."

Damn it, was he laughing at her? She was *not* going to be his source of amusement just because she didn't measure up to Annie Oakley in his eyes.

"I know you're not kidnapping me and I'm not spooked," she said between gritted teeth. Chloe tried to dig in her heels and found that it was a totally futile act. "But I do want to know where you're taking me."

Chance spared her a glance over his shoulder. "It's not what you think," he assured her calmly, wanting her to know that he had no intentions of getting physical with her in any way.

The problem was, it *was* the first thing that came to her mind. She instinctively knew that Chance was an honorable man, that he wouldn't just drag her off somewhere in order to have his way with her. He just wasn't that sort of person. But even so, she could feel her cheeks getting flushed, heating up and turning a deep shade of red that by no stretch of the imagination was her natural shade.

"Okay," Chloe retorted. "Then you tell me what to think."

She didn't expect him to laugh at that, but he did. "Oh, I doubt very much that there's a man alive who could do that, Chloe."

Maybe she *was* a woman who couldn't be told what to think, but if she was as independent as Chance was giving her credit for, she would have never allowed him to drag her out of her quarters in the first place.

Fueled by that thought, she demanded again, "Where are you taking me?"

"Some place where you can get rid of your inhibitions," he told her simply as he continued to pull her along behind him.

Okay, he was beginning to make her nervous. *Was* he taking her somewhere so that he could—that they could—damn it, how could she be so wrong about a person?

Nervous, incensed, she finally did manage to dig her heels into the ground, making him come to an abrupt stop. When he turned to look at her quizzically, she informed him in no uncertain terms, "I don't want to get rid of my 'inhibitions.'"

"Sure you do," he contradicted. She was about to yank her hand out of his and make a run for the main house when he went on to say, "No self-respecting Texan wants people to think that they can't ride."

"Can't ride?" she echoed. Panic and anger evaporated instantly. "This is about *riding*?" she questioned.

"Not exactly," he amended. "This is about teaching you the fundamentals of riding and ultimately getting you on the back of a horse. If that goes well," he continued, a hint of a smile curving his lips, "then we'll let Mirabel move a little with you on her back and we can call it 'riding' if anyone asks."

He led her to the stables, and when they entered, Chance let go of her hand. There was no need to continue pulling her in his wake. Turning around to face her, he told Chloe honestly, "And if you're going to ask me why I'm doing this, it's because I saw the look on your face earlier."

She didn't know what he was talking about. "What look?"

"The one that you had when you admitted to the boys that you didn't know how to ride. I figured it really bothered you more than you were willing to say. And when something winds up bothering you that much," he told her, bringing her over to Mirabel's stall, "you've got to do something about it or it'll just wind up haunting you." His eyes met hers for a moment. "I know all about things haunting a person," he told her. "Trust me, it's not a good thing."

He cleared his throat, as if that was enough to chase away the emotion that he had accidentally unearthed. He'd gotten very good at blocking out unwanted feelings—except in the middle of the night, when he had no control over them.

He forced himself to focus on Chloe. "Now, take it from me. There's no more peaceful place in the whole world than on the back of a horse, and the sooner you find that out for yourself, the better you're going to feel about the whole experience," he promised.

She was surprised to see that the mare was saddled, as if she was about to be taken out for a ride. Had Chance been that sure that he was going to get her to come here at this hour?

"And we have to do this now?" she asked him.

In response, he offered her that easygoing, sexy smile that transformed his uncompromising expression into a very compelling one. "No time like the present," he told her.

"Oh, I can think of plenty of other times," she assured Chance. She was doing her very best to hide her nervousness.

Despite her efforts, he saw right through them. Instead of making him feel sorry for her, or stopping him from continuing, it just urged him on. "Which is why this is the best time," he assured her.

The cowboy's reasoning completely mystified her. "How do you figure that?"

"The sooner you get over being afraid of riding," he explained patiently, "the sooner you'll be able to actually ride. And in no time at all, you'll find yourself wondering what the big deal was and what took you so long to get to it."

Chloe looked as if she was trying very hard not to be nervous, and he felt for her, but he also knew that what he'd just told her was true. She needed to meet this fear of hers head-on. He'd learned that firsthand. When he'd first returned to the States, all he'd wanted to do was go off into the wilderness and avoid people altogether. Separation, isolation—he realized that he just wanted to be alone to try and escape from the memories that plagued him of the death and devastation he'd seen. Loss of friends he'd served with, day in and day out had worn his soul to the breaking point—and yet he knew that logically he couldn't completely withdraw from society. He'd compromised by taking ranching jobs but never staying in any one place too long.

For his part, he couldn't see being afraid of riding, but then, except when he was stationed overseas, horses had always been a part of his life. It was like being afraid of the family dog.

"Give me your hand," he told her.

Instead of complying, she did just the opposite and pulled it behind her back.

"Why?" she wanted to know.

"Because I need a third hand," he quipped. Then his expression softened a little. "Just give it to me," he coaxed. "I promise this won't hurt."

Letting out a shaky breath, Chloe hesitantly put out her hand. He took it, covering it with his own, and guided it up to softly stroke the mare's muzzle.

"See, nothing to it," he told her, watching her expression. He was pleased to see her relax a little. Disengaging his hand from hers, Chance said, "Now you do it."

Holding her breath, Chloe did as he instructed, moving her fingertips lightly along the mare's coat. When Mirabel unexpectedly shook her head from side to side, as if tossing her mane, Chloe suppressed a gasp as she pulled her hand back.

"It's okay," Chance assured her. "Mirabel is a horse, not a statue. She's bound to make a few unexpected movements every now and then. She's not rejecting you. She's probably just inhaled something that's tickling her nose."

He paused a moment, allowing Chloe to regroup. "Now try it again," he urged.

It was meant as a suggestion, but to Chloe it sounded just like an order. Orders made her bristle. Still, she didn't want to come across like a coward in his eyes, so she put her hand on the mare's muzzle again and stroked it.

This time, the mare held still.

A smile lit up Chance's penetrating eyes. "See, that wasn't so bad, was it?"

"No," she admitted almost grudgingly, then added, "that was kind of nice."

She wasn't prepared for his question. "Think you'd like to get up on her?" he asked.

Her eyes widened. "You mean like ride her?"

Chance heard the nervousness in her voice and was quick to put her fears to rest. "No, I mean get up into her saddle and just sit still. We're not going anywhere just yet," he told her.

Standing beside the mare, Chloe looked up, judging where she would be sitting. She felt her stomach tightening.

"It's awfully high up," she said. "What if Mirabel decides to take off?"

"Her days of crashing through stable walls are definitely behind her." The second he assured her of that, he realized that Chloe thought he was being serious. "I'm kidding," he told her. "She's never crashed through a stable wall—or anything else for that matter. I'll help you up," he offered.

Chloe really didn't want to do this, but once she looked into Chance's eyes, she had the unerring feeling that he would keep her safe—even high up on a horse. So, reluctantly, she said, "Okay," and had him help.

Chance talked her through it, physically guiding her when he had to. He had her put her foot into the stirrup, then coaxed her through the steps until she swung her leg up over the mare's hind quarters, finally managing to get her other foot into the stirrup.

"You're doing fine," he told her.

"How come I don't feel fine?" Chloe challenged.

Probably because she looked stiff as a board, he thought.

"I've got an idea," he told her.

"I can get off the horse now?" Chloe asked him hopefully.

"No," he told her.

She didn't have very long to wait to see what he was up to. He took hold of the reins and in one fluid movement pulled himself up onto the horse directly behind her.

"What are you doing?" she cried, starting to turn in the saddle and then abruptly stopping because she was brushing up against Chance.

"My best to make you feel safer," he replied.

Having Chance so close that she could feel the heat from his chest against her back made her feel a whole host of sensations—but "safer" definitely wasn't one of them.

Chapter Nine

He needed some air. Right now, the scent of Chloe's shampoo was filling up his senses and making him think and feel things he shouldn't be thinking *or* feeling. If he didn't get moving, he was liable to do something one of them was going to regret.

For a moment, in an act of self-preservation, Chance had considered just going ahead and guiding the mare outside. But he had a feeling that it was in the best interests of both of them if he asked her first. He thought it would be better if Chloe was prepared rather than just springing things on her. She seemed to be jumpy enough against him as it was.

"So," he asked her, "are you game?"

For the life of her, Chloe didn't know exactly what he was asking her. She knew what she *wanted* Chance to be asking her, but that would be leaving herself wide open for all sorts of complications that she knew she just couldn't handle.

"Game for what?" she asked uneasily.

"To take a little ride."

"And do what?" she asked suspiciously.

"Ride?" It was more of a question because he didn't know what she was expecting to hear, or what she wanted him to say.

"Oh. How far?"

She felt him shrug against her back. "I thought just around the outside of the stable for tonight. Next time we'll go farther—and on separate horses," he added. She heard the amusement in his voice. And then he asked, "Ready?"

Chloe was ready, all right. To jump off the horse and run back to her cottage. But for some reason she nodded her assent. Whom was she kidding? It wasn't the horse she wasn't ready for. It was Chance.

She wasn't ready to have his arms tighten around her as he took control of the reins, to feel his warm breath on her neck as he coaxed the mare out of the stable, to feel his muscled thighs around hers as they rode the perimeter of the corral. Not at all ready.

Suddenly the evening seemed to get too warm, and she had to steel herself against this man wrapped around her.

"You all right?" he asked her. "You're as stiff as a board."

She gave him the first excuse that came into her head. "Just trying not to fall off."

"You can't fall off," he pointed out. "I have you, and besides, Mirabel isn't exactly trotting. If she were going any slower, she'd be going backward."

Up against him the way she was, she couldn't get comfortable. It would mean lowering her guard, and she couldn't afford to do that. "I had no idea the corral was this large," she commented.

"It's not really. It just seems that way because we're moving around it at a snail's pace. We can go faster," Chance offered, pretending to get ready to kick his heels into the mare's flanks to make her pick up her pace.

"No, no," Chloe protested, raising a hand as if that somehow made her plea more emphatic. "This pace is just fine. Unless you mind," she added, suddenly realizing that riding like this had to be immensely boring to someone like Chance. Given this speed, any second now he was liable to fall asleep.

Mind? Chance thought, astonished that she should phrase it that way. Why would he mind having his arms around a beautiful woman, holding her a hair's breadth away from him?

Being here like this with Chloe reminded him that it had been a long, long time since he had allowed himself to get physically close to someone without worrying about the resulting consequences.

"No, I'm just fine," he assured her. "Matter of fact," he told her as they approached the stable door, "we can go around again if you'd like."

Yes, she'd "like"—which was just the problem. With very little effort, she could just close her eyes and transport herself to another place in time, a time when everything seemed right in the world.

A time when she fantasized about the future that lay ahead of her. A future that included the husband she loved and a family. Having Chance hold her like this made it so easy for her to remember—so easy to yearn.

She had to stop doing that, she silently upbraided herself.

It was time to stop dreaming and face reality—a reality that included neither her husband nor a family.

"No, that's all right," she told him. "Once is enough for now—if you don't mind. We both have things to do," she added, being deliberately vague.

"I don't," he told her honestly. Lord, but she smelled good, even out here with the night air diluting the mind-numbing scent that was still lingering in her hair. "This is the guys' free time," he pointed out, explaining, "They're either doing homework or just kicking back. After I check in on them, the rest of my evening is wide open," he told her.

"Oh, well, mine isn't."

What was with her? Two lies in one day? But she absolved herself of the guilt over this last one. It was self-preservation. She simply couldn't be around Chance in her vulnerable state. There was just something about having him close to her like this with the dusk slipping into nightfall that made her uneasy. Not because she thought that Chance might try something but because she was afraid that *she* might.

"I have to get back," she told him.

"Sure, I understand."

He wasn't about to make things difficult for her, and he certainly wasn't about to press her for details. The last thing he wanted was to make Chloe feel as if he was encroaching on her space or trying to box her in in any sort of way.

After bringing the mare back into the stable, Chance dismounted, then turned to face Chloe and offered her his assistance to get down.

Chloe hesitated, but she knew that she wasn't in any position to attempt a graceful dismount. Not yet. Because she had absolutely no idea how. So she took the arms that were being offered to her and allowed Chance to help her down.

That maneuver involved getting very close to him for another very long moment.

A moment in which her heart seemed to stop even as her pulse accelerated to double time.

Chance picked her up off the mare and brought her down, holding her by the waist and sliding the length of her body down a hint away from his until her feet were finally touching the ground.

He was holding her close enough for her imagination to vividly take flight—and to silently lament when he finally withdrew his hands from around her waist.

When she opened her mouth to thank him, Chloe found that she couldn't speak. Her mouth had completely gone dry, and her words stuck to the roof of her mouth.

Swallowing, she gave communication another try. This time, she did something more than just croak. "Thank you for the lesson."

Chance laughed shortly. "I'd hardly call that a lesson."

"Okay, have it your way," she allowed. "Thank you for the introduction…to horseback riding," she added belatedly, realizing it might sound as if she was thanking him for something entirely different.

"My pleasure," he told her.

It was only after she'd turned from him and began to hurriedly walk away, back to the guesthouse, that she heard him call after her, saying, "This isn't over, you know. I intend to give you that riding lesson."

"When I have time," she tossed over her shoulder without even looking back.

She wasn't about to make promises. She'd had enough of that.

"*Make* time."

It wasn't a suggestion; it was clearly an order.

His order rang in her ears as she all but ran the rest of the way to the guesthouse.

Chance remained outside longer than he knew he should have, watching her and admiring Chloe's form until she was gone from sight.

Nothing wrong with that, Chance told himself as he turned away and went back into the stable. *Just admiring one of the Lord's finer creations, nothing more than that*.

And he would continue telling himself that, Chance thought, until it finally stuck.

"Something on your mind?" Sasha asked her the next day.

Graham's wife had sat in on one of Chloe's sessions with Ryan and then another session with Brandon.

Chloe knew she had to be sporadically supervised, especially since she was so new to Peter's Place. But she still couldn't help being a little nervous.

Added to that was the fact that she kept expecting Chance to come walking in at any moment, announcing that he was going to give her another lesson. Right now it felt as if the last of her nerves had been worn down to a tiny nub. She felt so tense inside that if she were a guitar string, she would have snapped in half.

But she was trying her very best not to appear that way on the surface.

Judging by Sasha's question she wasn't succeeding very well.

"No," she replied, trying to sound laid-back. "Other than doing right by these boys," Chloe qualified at the last moment.

Sasha smiled. "Nice answer but not the one I was looking for." She leaned forward in her chair. "I mean, is there anything else going on? You seem like you're waiting for something to happen."

Obviously, being an undercover spy was never going to be an option for her, Chloe thought.

"No," she denied again. And then she decided to own up a little, hoping that would be enough for Sasha. "I guess being observed puts me on edge a little. I realize that I'm not as good as you are at this, but—"

"Nobody's comparing us," Sasha told her firmly. "We all have our own individual styles. I'm just here to observe whether or not you're connecting with the boys—and I'm happy to say that you are."

The truth was, Chloe was somewhat nervous about

measuring up to the woman who had hired her. After all, these had initially been "Sasha's boys" and in a sense, they still were. She'd been rather afraid that both the boys and Sasha would view her as an interloper.

"You don't know how happy it makes me to hear you say that," Chloe told her.

"Then it's mutual," Sasha told her with a warm smile. "Because it makes me very happy to honestly be able to say that." Sasha looked at her a little more closely. "But are you sure there's nothing else? You don't need some time off, do you?"

"Time off?" Chloe echoed. "I just got here." She felt as if she was just beginning to get the hang of the routine. "I've still got a long ways to go before I make a niche at Peter's Place. Why would I want to take some time off?"

Sasha shrugged. "To acclimate yourself to the area a little more. This is different from living in the city," she said sympathetically.

"Amen to that," Chloe said with a laugh. "It's almost too quiet here at night to sleep, but I'm slowly getting used to that, too."

"So you're settling in?" Sasha asked.

"Absolutely," Chloe told her with feeling.

"I'm glad because I can't tell you how nice it is to have another woman around. I mean, I have the girls," she said, referring to her two daughters, "and I love them to pieces, but it'll be a lot of years before either one of them is anywhere near being someone I can actually talk to." She quickly amended, "I mean, Graham is a wonderful man and he's really great with the girls, but well, you know men, there's a lot they don't understand when it comes to the way we women feel."

Smiling at her, Sasha put her hand over Chloe's.

"I just want you to know that if you ever need to just talk—about nothing or about something—I'm here for you."

When Chloe couldn't help but laugh, Sasha looked at her a little uncertainly, wanting to be let in on the joke. "Did I just say something funny?"

"Not exactly." The whole thing struck her as rather ironic. "What you just said to me is what I told all four of the boys after I had my first session with each of them."

"Well, my offer was rendered from a nonprofessional position," Sasha said. "As a friend," she further qualified. And then she continued. "And as a friend, I have to say that being around you right now reminds me of that old adage, the one about being a cat on a hot tin roof."

"I make you think of that?" Chloe asked, secretly wondering if the same thing had occurred to Brandon and Ryan, the two boys she'd seen today for their sessions.

"Well, not exactly," Sasha admitted. "But certainly close to that. Tell me, are you waiting for something to happen, or for someone? Or is it just that I make you very nervous?"

"*You* don't make me nervous," Chloe quickly told her. How could she tell her boss that it was Chance who made her nervous?

It was time to be truthful with herself. To admit that she wasn't afraid of the riding lesson he intended to give her—or the horse—although she wasn't exactly confidence personified when it came to either. What had her feeling so internally jumpy was the man. And the prospect of her next interaction with him.

Her next *solo* interaction with him, she silently emphasized.

Interacting with Chance when there were others around was fine. They were just two employees at Peter's Place with the same prime focus: getting the teens assigned to the ranch to find their better inner core.

She could go on working alongside Chance all day like that.

It was the anticipation of being alone with him that had her acting like that so-called restless cat Sasha had just likened her to. Because being alone with Chance woke things up within her that were better off left dormant and sleeping.

She was certainly better off if they were left dormant and sleeping, Chloe thought.

Looking at Sasha now, she realized that the woman was still waiting for some sort of response from her as to why she was acting so unsettled.

Sasha seemed almost *hungry* for some sort of shared confidence, Chloe thought. She supposed that it was almost cruel of her not to say *something*, even though it was against the privacy she tried so desperately to maintain.

Taking a breath, Chloe made her decision. She'd confide in her half brother's wife. Maybe then they could move past this and get on with her work at Peter's Place.

"Chance wants to give me riding lessons," she told Sasha.

The other woman's face literally lit up.

Chapter Ten

"Oh, really?" Sasha asked. If possible, she sat up even a little straighter, her interest unwaveringly engaged. Delight was all but vibrating in her voice.

"Yes," Chloe replied. Her voice was as quiet as Sasha's was vibrant and enthused.

"You don't know how to ride a horse?" Sasha questioned, clearly surprised.

Chloe shrugged. Not wanting to get into a discussion about that, she just said, "The opportunity never came up."

For a second, Sasha was quiet and Chloe thought that, mercifully, that was the end of the discussion on that topic. But then Sasha looked at her, her smile even wider than it had been a moment ago, her eyes dancing.

She clapped her hands together. "This is wonderful!" the woman exclaimed.

"I wouldn't exactly go that far," Chloe protested, not really sure why her newly discovered sister-in-law would be so happy to find out that there was this definite gap in her education. "It just...*is*," she finally said.

This was what she got for trying to be completely honest, Chloe thought a second later. Rather than moving on, she had the feeling that she was about to get sucked down in the ocean by the undertow.

If the gleeful look of anticipation on Sasha's face— the origin of which was a complete mystery to her— wasn't enough, Chance picked that exact moment to walk into the room.

The man had awful timing, Chloe thought, feeling her stomach tighten at the same time that there was this sinking sensation right in the center of it. She was definitely a woman torn.

"Speak of the devil," Sasha declared, amusement as well as pleasure surrounding every syllable that she uttered.

Chance looked just a little taken aback. "Since when have I become the devil?" he asked uncertainly, not quite sure what he'd just walked in on.

Sasha rose from her chair. The binder she'd brought in with her to make notes while observing Chloe's session was in her hands and pressed up against her chest.

"We were just talking about you," she said dismissively. "Well, I'm sure I hear Maddie calling for me so I'll just leave the two of you to it," she said.

Chloe shifted self-consciously. Sasha had all but held up a sign with instructions on it as to what she thought they should do next once she left and they were alone.

One of Chance's eyebrows arched as he turned to regard the woman who was left standing in the room.

"'To it?'" he asked Chloe, torn between being bemused and confused.

"I told Sasha you offered to give me riding lessons." Chloe cleared her throat. She couldn't remember when she had ever felt more awkward. "Sasha thought it was a good idea."

"Oh." He nodded as if comprehending what he had just walked in on—except that Chloe wasn't 100 percent convinced that he wasn't reading a great deal more into Sasha's comment. "Well, it is a good idea," he told her. "Everyone should know how to ride."

"I would think it's more a matter of preference," Chloe countered. "It's not like it's a life-or-death situation, like learning to swim."

Chance wasn't about to get into an involved discussion on the subject. He had a far simpler way to resolve it.

"Wouldn't you rather know how to do something than not know how to do it?"

Chloe suppressed a sigh. She supposed that Chance did have a point. And she didn't want him to think that she was reluctant to broaden her horizons.

"Sure."

She stood up, telling herself she was making way too big a deal out of this. Chance was just giving her a simple horseback riding lesson—same as what he was hired to do with the boys. She had to stop feeling so nervous about it.

So nervous about him.

A thought suddenly occurred to her. "Are you going to be teaching me to ride in the corral?"

Chance hadn't given it much thought. "Yes. That's where I've been doing it with the boys. Why? Would you rather not have your lesson there?" he asked, sensing her reluctance.

She avoided making eye contact with him as she spoke, not wanting to see amusement or something even more demoralizing in his eyes.

"I'd rather we didn't have an audience," she confessed. "Is there any place else that we could go for these lessons?"

"Sure. It's a big ranch," he reminded her. "I just thought you'd rather get your first lessons somewhere where you felt safe."

That was when she finally looked at him. "Why wouldn't I feel safe somewhere else?" she asked him.

"The corral's contained. If I give you riding lessons out in the open, I figure you'd worry that Mirabel could get it into her head to just run off with you on her back."

"Oh." Enlightenment came to her riding a thunderbolt. He wasn't talking about her feeling safer in the corral because she felt he wouldn't try to kiss her in broad daylight in front of possible witnesses. He was talking about the mare running off with her. "You've got the faster horse, don't you?" she asked.

"No disrespect meant for Mirabel, but yes, I do. By quite a lot when you come right down to it."

This time her eyes didn't leave his when she responded. "Then if something happens, say, to spook Mirabel, you could catch up to me on your horse, couldn't you?"

"If it came to that, yes. But from what I've been told, Mirabel doesn't spook easily. That's one of the reasons why I picked her for you."

She believed him. "Then I'd rather you took me somewhere where no one else can watch and see how bad I am at this."

"You're not bad at riding," he told her. "You just need to learn the right techniques, that's all. It's not all that hard." He tried to soothe her, but he could see his words weren't working. "But if you feel that strongly about it, I know this quiet clearing not too far from the lake that'll do just fine for our purposes."

A quiet clearing by the lake sounded as if it would do fine for other purposes, too, Chloe thought. But she kept that to herself, hoping that the same idea hadn't occurred to him.

Because the lake was some distance from the corral, Chance decided to take her there on his horse. He told Chloe that right now it was safer for her if they rode double on his horse.

"What about Mirabel?" Chloe asked, wanting to be clear on the logistics. "Isn't she coming, too?"

"She'll be right behind us," he explained. "I'll just hold on to her reins so she doesn't get it into her head to hang back."

"And your horse won't mind?" she asked, looking at the black stallion that Chance had already saddled and was waiting for them in the stable. Mirabel was in the next stall, saddled, as well.

Chance unconsciously furrowed his brow. He wasn't sure he understood her question. "Mind what?"

"That we're both going to be riding on him at the same time?" She looked at the stallion doubtfully, worried about the extra weight.

Chance laughed, tickled by what she was innocently suggesting. "He's fine with it," he told her. "He's not the jealous sort."

Chloe flushed. When he said it out loud like that, she realized that she sounded like an idiot. "I didn't mean…"

He was quick to try to save her from embarrassment. "I know what you meant. C'mon, we're wasting daylight," he urged. "Or was that the idea?" he asked, pretending to look at her as if the light had suddenly dawned on him.

"No," Chloe denied quickly. She wound up sounding almost breathless.

He was going to have to tread lightly with this one, Chance thought. Most of the time, he preferred to keep to himself and not bother interacting with people. It saved time and saved him from spinning his wheels. But he had to admit there was something about this woman that had burrowed under his skin.

He liked seeing the way her eyes flashed and the way she tossed her hair when she was digging in and being stubborn. But for all that, Chloe made him think that he was dealing with a vulnerable, wounded bird.

The whole thing was a revelation to him, he thought.

He had never realized until just now that he had any desire to protect a wounded bird.

Or that he rather liked it.

Maybe his soul hadn't died on the battlefield after all.

"Then we'd better get going," he told her. "Come on. Let's get you up there."

The next moment, while Chloe was absently regarding just how much taller his stallion appeared in comparison with her mare, she felt strong hands come around her waist. Suddenly, she was airborne.

As her breath caught in her throat, Chance had her in the saddle in a matter of seconds. She barely had time to suppress the cry of surprise that had all but escaped from her lips.

And then, the next moment, there he was, right behind her. *Snuggly* right behind her, she couldn't help noticing as his body seemed to fit perfectly against hers.

A multitude of sensations went zipping through Chloe, some familiar, some brand-new, all unsettling.

A riding lesson, this is just a riding lesson, she silently insisted.

There was no need for her to react like this to *any* of this. Chance was just doing her a favor, teaching her how to ride so she could go out with the boys. She had to think of it in that light, she told herself.

And *only* in that light.

Chance brought his arms around her, picking up his horse's reins as he formed a protective circle around her.

"You all right?" he asked.

"I'm fine," she answered. *If you don't count the fact*

*that my heart is just about ready to break the sound
barrier.*

She felt Chance leaning into her. Her heart raced a
little harder.

The next moment he was whispering into her ear.
"I guarantee that you'll feel a whole lot better if you
breathe."

"Right. Breathing," she agreed the next second.

And then, just to prove that she had heard Chance,
she went on to elaborately do just that.

Chloe really didn't remember the journey to the
clearing, at least, not when she thought if it in terms
of miles or scenery. All she was aware of was how the
gentle back-and-forth rocking of the stallion caused
Chance's body to move seductively against hers. She
was concentrating so hard on not reacting to him that
she didn't even realize when they'd reached their des-
tination.

"We're here," Chance announced.

The next second, without any warning, Chance was
dismounting. Abruptly deprived of his support and
thinking something had gone wrong, Chloe quickly
turned to look down at him and wound up nearly tum-
bling out of the saddle.

"Hey, no sudden trick moves until after I'm satisfied that you know how to ride. We don't want to rush
you off to the nearest doctor." He looked up at her face.
She'd turned almost completely pale. "Hey, are you all
right?" he asked, concerned. "I was just kidding."

"I knew that," Chloe mumbled although she clearly didn't.

"Good." He didn't believe her for a second. Chance extended his arms up to her and said, "Let's get you down from there." Taking hold of her waist, he eased her down until her feet were back on the ground. "This is the last time I'm going to help you dismount," he told her. "I'll teach you and then you're on your own."

He saw the apprehensive look that crept over her face. Rather than being off-putting, he thought she looked even more adorable.

"Don't worry," he assured her. "You'll do fine."

"I wasn't worried," she informed him perhaps a little too quickly.

He graciously accepted her protest, even though he felt he knew otherwise. "My mistake."

Bringing Mirabel closer to Chloe, he announced, "Okay. This is lesson number one."

And so it began.

Chance patiently kept at it for the next four hours, verbally diagramming every move he wanted her to make so precisely that after a little while, Chloe forgot to be nervous.

Progress came by tiny inches—but it came.

At the end of the session Chloe had a good handle on the basics. He'd taught her how to fluidly mount her horse and how to dismount, as well. He'd taught her how to give the most basic commands to the animal so that the mare knew when she was expected to go and when to stop.

Through it all Chance didn't raise his voice or lose his temper, nor did he easily dispense praise, either.

He did, however, let her know if she was doing something wrong so that she wouldn't repeat it. On the few occasions that she did repeat her mistake, he patiently reviewed the steps again, and had her go through the paces over and over until she got it right.

And then, finally, when she thought she was never going to see it again, it happened.

Chance smiled.

"I think that's it for today," he told her.

She was exhausted and so ready to go home, but even so, she had to ask him. "That bad?"

"That good," Chance corrected.

Her eyes fairly danced as she asked, "Really?"

"Really," he echoed. "And our next session is going to be in the corral," he informed her, "because you have nothing to be ashamed of. Now, for your reward, I want to take you to see something that a lot of people live out their whole lives without ever being able to see or appreciate."

"Oh? What?"

The nervousness was back in her voice, Chance thought. But he knew just how to put it to rest. Taking her hand, he led her over to the lake.

"Look," he said, pointing out what he wanted her to see.

Once again, Chloe's breath caught in her throat.

Chapter Eleven

Chance was right. It was glorious.

Chloe had seen sunsets before. They were, after all, a part of everyday life. But she'd never seen one like this.

Standing there with him, at the edge of the lake, she looked up at the sky.

And promptly had her breath stolen away.

There was a multitude of muted colors reaching out to the heavens, as if the sun was having one last hurrah before finally retreating into the dusk and then the darkness, where it would wait for dawn and a rebirth.

"I never get tired of seeing this," Chance told her. "Makes me realize how really beautiful nature is. It also makes me feel that no matter how bad things might seem, in the scheme of things, everything is going to be all right."

Listening to him, Chloe could appreciate the noble sentiment—as well as the man who uttered it. "It is magnificent."

Maybe it *was* the sunset that did it. Or maybe it was standing here so close to Chance, being infused with a sense of peace she hadn't felt in a long time.

Maybe it was all of the above.

Chloe couldn't honestly pinpoint the reason. All she knew was that when she turned toward Chance, she felt this undeniable, incredible pull within her. Pulling her toward him.

It kept her transfixed so that when Chance lowered his head, bringing his lips close to hers, she didn't move. Didn't breathe.

Didn't do anything—except will the moment to go on forever.

Her wish increased tenfold when he finally kissed her.

The moment their lips met, she could feel something explode within her. Something gleeful and joyous, as if she had been holding her breath, waiting for this to happen from the first moment she'd met him.

Hoping this would happen, she realized.

And yet, it surprised her.

Surprised her that Chance kissed her. What surprised her even more was that she actually *felt* something rather than just the deadness that had existed within her ever since she'd first found out that Donnie was never coming back to her.

Chloe could sense her heart slip into a wild double-time beat when Chance deepened the kiss, when his arms went around her waist and pulled her flush against him.

Almost breathless, she laced her arms around his neck, leaning into Chance as well as into his kiss. The sun might have been setting over the lake, but right now, it felt as if it was bursting out from within her, sending out long sunbeams to every single part of her.

She was certain that if Chance opened his eyes, he would see her glowing in the dark.

Chance wasn't sure just what had come over him. Yes, it was a beautiful sunset, and yes, he was here sharing it with a beautiful woman, but that alone wasn't enough for him to do what he was doing. They worked together, and he firmly believed that it was never a good idea to mix work with pleasure.

Since he'd come back from the service, he'd been a loner and the first to admit that things ultimately had a habit of not working out in these sorts of situations. When that happened, they wound up turning awkward. He made it a point to never stay in any one place for long, moving on when he grew restless, and he knew that he could do that here, too.

But there was something about this place, about the work that was being done, that appealed to him. That *spoke* to him. Peter's Place was a place he could believe in and for the first time in a long time, he found himself wanting to be a part of it, not just in a cursory way but in a way that actually mattered. That made a difference.

He wanted to make a difference.

That was all the more reason for not getting involved with a woman who worked here, he argued with himself. But again, there was just something about Chloe that reached right into his gut and grabbed him. Something that made him want to protect her, want to be her hero and want to make her smile.

Heaven knew that right now, *she* was making him smile. Not only that, but it had been a very long time since kissing a girl had actually rocked his world, and she was certainly doing that right now for him.

So much so that he shed his common sense like a snake shed its skin and continued doing exactly what he had been doing.

Chance tightened his arms around her, getting lost in the kiss he had initiated. Getting lost in the sweet, heady fragrance he always detected whenever he was standing anywhere close to Chloe.

He could feel himself wanting her.

If she were any other woman who had crossed his path for the evening, he might have gone on to see where this would lead. But he instinctively knew that Chloe wasn't someone meant for a casual coupling— or even a torrid one. Chloe was the kind of woman a guy brought home to his mother—if he had a mother.

But for him that hadn't been the case for a long time now, he thought. His mother had died six months after he'd graduated high school. His father had died in a hunting accident years before that. Being on his own and alone had been a way of life for him and he'd made his peace with that.

Until now.

He didn't have to be told that Chloe could be easily hurt, and he already sensed that she *had* been hurt—

badly—by something or someone. There was pain in her eyes when he looked into them, even when she was laughing at something. He wasn't about to add to that pain. He didn't need that on his conscience.

But he knew that if he continued kissing her like this, he was definitely going to want more, and he also knew that if he pushed, even just a little, he could convince her to make love with him.

But that's not how he wanted it to happen.

And that wouldn't be fair to her. So, hard though it was for him, Chance forced himself to draw his mouth away from hers.

His heart still hammering wildly, he made himself take a step back, although he still kept his arms around her waist, wanting to take comfort in that contact for just a moment longer.

Chloe's eyes sought his, and he saw the question in them. Why had he stopped? He also felt her shudder as she tried to catch her breath.

Chance was coping with a few struggles of his own. He wasn't accustomed to abruptly stopping like this once he'd started kissing a woman. But he knew he had to.

"I think we should be getting back before Graham sends out a search party to come looking for us."

The sun had all but set, taking almost all of the available light with it. But there was still just enough left for him to see that her cheeks had grown appealingly pink.

Had he embarrassed her by kissing her? Or embarrassed her by stopping? He couldn't tell.

"We wouldn't want that," she agreed. She kept her

face averted as they walked back to their tree-tethered horses. "Thanks for the riding lesson," she told him, trying to sound casual. "And for sharing the sunset."

Chance laughed softly. "Not exactly mine to keep," he told her. "The sunset," he explained when he saw her looking at him quizzically. "As for the riding lesson, that was my pleasure." Mindful of her still-limited experience, he helped her mount, then swung onto his own horse. "But remember, you're not off the hook yet. I still have a little more to teach you."

As they headed back to the ranch, Chloe felt her thoughts—and her pulse—race. Maybe she was just reading things into what Chance had said, or maybe that kiss they'd shared had changed her focus. Whatever the reason, Chloe caught herself thinking that Chance had a great deal to teach her and riding was only a small part of it.

What's the matter with you? she upbraided herself as they continued riding to the main house. *One kiss and you're ready to forget about Donnie? Forget about what you had with Donnie?*

A shaft of guilt at her disloyalty to her husband's memory shot through her. How could she let herself get carried away like that?

Besides, that kiss probably didn't mean anything to Chance, she told herself. He was just taking advantage of an opportune moment, nothing more.

Just look at him, she thought, slanting a quick glance at him. The man was gorgeous, every woman's idea of the perfect cowboy. He undoubtedly had his pick of women, and that meant he had no need for a permanent relationship. Or any sort of a commitment.

Even if she was, by some wild chance, ready to allow herself to get carried away and start being serious about Chance, she knew she was bound to be hurt.

And the very last thing her heart needed was to be bruised. She already had gone through enough pain to last her a lifetime. There was absolutely no way she was going to set herself up to be hurt ever again—even if Chance was inclined to get involved with her, which she was willing to bet he wasn't.

She had a strong feeling that relationships weren't for him. The man was a loner. He'd all but told her so the first time they'd met.

No, she argued as they rode back, what happened at the lake was an aberration. A lovely aberration, but still just an aberration. And there wasn't going to be a sequel—ever—she told herself.

By now they had reached the ranch and were nearing the stable. Chloe was more than ready to call it a night.

But Chance had other ideas.

"You're not done yet," he told her.

She had no idea what to expect as she finally forced herself to look in his direction. "Oh?"

"I might have saddled Mirabel for you, but now it's time for you to learn how to take care of her. There's more to working with a horse than just riding it," Chance told her as he led the way into the stable. "So, since you're through riding her for the day, you have to unsaddle her. It's like when you were little and had to put away your toys when you were finished playing with them," he added, hoping the metaphor would help her get the idea.

There was just one thing wrong with his analogy, she thought, and she told him so. "I didn't have any toys when I was little."

That piece of information caught him by surprise. Just how poor had she been? At that moment it occurred to Chance that he really knew very little about this woman whom he found himself attracted to.

"No toys? None? Really?" he asked. After all, he knew that she was Graham's half sister. He'd just assumed that all the Fortunes were well cared for. But since there was no reason for her to lie, maybe she'd had it rougher than he'd thought. His heart—a heart he'd thought he'd forfeited on the battlefields of a foreign land—went out to her as he listened.

"Well, I did have one," she admitted. "I had a stuffed bear—Theodore," she told him, recalling the bear's name. "And I took Theodore everywhere, so I guess you might say that I never stopped playing with him. And since I didn't, I never put him away."

"What happened to Theodore?" he asked, curious.

He watched, fascinated, as a fond, faraway smile curved her lips. "I loved him to death and eventually, he just fell apart."

He dismounted before putting his horse in his stall. Chloe followed suit, and he came to join her.

"I guess then being loved by you comes with a price," he said.

She knew Chance just meant it as a joke, but the

comment had her thinking of Donnie. And aching—
on two counts.

"I guess so," she said quietly.

Her tone made him realize that he'd blundered.
Chance quickly changed the subject to something more
neutral.

"Because you're new at this, I'm going to walk you
through it this time. But from now on, when we go riding, you'll have to saddle and unsaddle Mirabel—or
any other horse if you decide to go on to a more lively
one," he added.

There was no chance of that happening, Chloe
thought. "Mirabel is lively enough for me, thank you,"
she told him. She was grateful to Chance for switching
subjects. "And I'll be happy to saddle her the next time
we go out—although I have to say that I'm not too sure
how happy Mirabel will be about it."

"You do it right and she'll be fine," he told her. "It's
not that complicated." And then he unconsciously went
into teaching mode. "Okay, you'll need to loosen the
cinch in order to get the saddle off."

"Loosen the cinch," Chloe repeated gamely, looking
at the saddle. She had no idea what the cinch looked like
or where it was located. Moreover, she was afraid if she
did the wrong thing, the mare was going to get skittish.
Biting the bullet, she asked, "And how do I do that?"

Chance laughed. "The cinch is right here."

Lifting the stirrup on Chloe's side, he pointed it out.
And then he walked her through the entire process,
narrating every move he made until he had the horse
standing in her stall, sans saddle, blanket and bridle.

He saw that Chloe looked as if she was ready to leave.

"Not yet," he warned her. "You're not finished."

Everything had been taken off the mare except for her horseshoes, Chloe thought. She couldn't see what else needed to be done.

"You going to put a nightgown on her?" she joked.

"No, but you're going to wipe her down—just in case she's wet." He saw that Chloe looked a little bemused. "You're familiar with the phrase 'Ridden hard and put away wet?'" he asked. Then, not waiting for a response, he told her, "Well, we don't do that around here.

"Just in case the horse is wet and the temperature drops at night, your horse might get a chill. No matter what you might have seen in the movies or on TV, horses are a lot more delicate than you might think. They come down with a lot of the same ailments that people do in addition to having their own set of diseases.

"You take care of your horse, and your horse will take care of you," Chance concluded, then stopped abruptly, catching himself. "Sorry, I was giving you the exact same lecture that I usually give the boys," he apologized.

He didn't want her thinking he was talking down to her. It was just that he really cared about the way the horses were treated. Though they were powerful animals, he thought of them as defenseless when it came to being on the receiving end of bad treatment. Any horse in his care had to be treated well.

"That's okay. I like it," she told him truthfully. "And I did learn something," she added.

He looked at her doubtfully. "Don't kiss up to me, Chloe," he told her.

She thought that was an odd phrase for him to use, given what had happened a while ago at the lake, but she let it go, other than to protest, "But I wasn't."

"Oh, in that case, good to hear." And then he handed her a brush with coarse dark bristles.

She looked at it, confused. "Are you telling me that my hair's a mess?"

Chance laughed. "No, I'm telling you to brush the horse."

"Is that part of the ritual?" There were certainly a lot of steps to remember when it came to taking care of a horse, she thought.

"No, but Mirabel likes it, and I thought having you brush her might help build a bond between you two." Since Chloe still looked just a bit perplexed as she contemplated the brush in her hand, he asked, "May I?"

Chloe was quick to surrender the brush. "Sure."

"You don't want to brush her too hard," he told her. "Just long, even strokes. Think of it like getting a massage."

That didn't help. She shook her head. "Never got one," Chloe told him. Then she looked at him curiously. "Have you?"

The very thought of it made him laugh. "I'm not exactly the beauty spa type," he told her. "I was just trying to find a way for you to be able to relate to the brushing."

Chloe took the brush from him and began to brush Mirabel's flanks. "Like this?"

"Almost." Chance covered her hand with his own and then slowly guided her through the first few strokes. "Like this," he told her, then continued to move her hand beneath his and along the horse.

She knew that technically all they were doing was brushing the horse's coat, but they were doing it in one joint motion, and somehow, it felt rather intimate that way.

She could feel her body heating up, the way it had at the lake when he'd kissed her.

She needed to maintain better control over herself than this, she silently lectured. And part of maintaining that control was not having him get so close to her.

She needed space.

Shrugging his hand off her own, she told him, "I think that I can take it from here now, Chance."

"Go for it," he told her, stepping back. He watched her for a few moments, and then he abruptly turned away and went into the next stall to take care of his own horse.

And to think about something else other than Chloe. Or try to.

Chapter Twelve

Chloe finally felt as if her life was slowly falling into place.

She was making decent headway with the four boys who were currently staying at the ranch, albeit at a different pace with each one. Initially, she'd felt as if all of the teens regarded her warily and were keeping up their defenses, but mercifully, that was all changing.

Jonah and Ryan had taken less time to come around than the other two. Since they had already made a bit of progress under Sasha's counseling, it didn't take them all that long to lower their guard and trust her. She was here a few weeks and they had begun to talk to her about things that were troubling them, as well as some things that they were trying to work out.

She found it rougher going with Brandon and Will.

Brandon didn't want to risk getting close to anyone because he was afraid of ultimately losing that contact, the way he had lost his brother. As for Will, although he clearly yearned for his mother, because of what she had done, he didn't trust any woman who entered his life.

Although their progress was at slower pace, seeing all four of the teens come around because of her efforts proved to be exceedingly gratifying for Chloe. She felt as if she was actually making a difference in their lives, which in turn added a great deal of significance to her own life. She felt it gave her a real purpose.

And then there were the riding lessons with Chance. She would have never thought, not in a million years, that she'd be proud of the headway she was making with that, but she was.

Chance turned out to be the consummate teacher, which really surprised her. She would have said at the outset of their association that teaching someone to ride wouldn't have made a difference to Chance one way or another. He had struck her as being the poster boy for the quintessential loner. But it turned out that Chance was nothing if not patient with her.

He was patient with the boys, too, she noted whenever she had the chance to observe them together. And she could see that they began to regard him as the father figure they'd lacked in their childhoods.

For that matter, she thought as she finished working on that day's notes and looked out the window at the corral where Chance worked with Will, in a way he was the father *she* had never known, as well.

Except, she reminded herself, she would have defi-

nitely never reacted to her father the way she was reacting to Chance.

Chloe sighed.

She was still rather uncertain about all that. Uncertain how she felt about having feelings for him.

She felt as if she was going around in circles.

"You think too much," she murmured to herself
under her breath.

But she couldn't help herself, couldn't help analyz-
ing, comparing—remembering. Remembering how it
felt to be in love with Donnie—and how that had all
ended so heartbreakingly.

Stop it, she upbraided herself. *Just enjoy whatever
happens as it happens. For heaven's sake, for once in
your life just float, don't plot.*

Chloe shook her head. Easier said than done.

She turned away from the window and went back
to her work.

Like a delayed reaction, it slowly dawned on Chance
that for the first time since he'd gotten back from serving overseas that he finally, *finally* had a renewed sense
of purpose. That was something that had eluded him
while he'd been in the military and certainly afterward,
when he'd returned stateside.

He supposed that was why he had subconsciously
drifted from ranch to ranch and job to job. He'd blamed
it on restlessness, but he now realized that he'd been
searching for a meaning to his life, some sort of a purpose. Working here, at Peter's Place, with its rescued

horses and its rescued kids, was giving him that sense of purpose.

And it felt damn good, Chance thought. The troubled teens he had been put in charge of had essentially come a long way in a short time. He knew in part that was because of Chloe and her sessions with them, but in part it was because of him, as well. And their noticeable evolution gave him a reason for getting up in the morning.

He never thought he'd ever feel that way again. For the longest time he'd believed that opening his eyes each morning, feeling as if his soul had been sucked out by forces he couldn't grapple with, couldn't untangle, was going to be his fate until the day he died.

Now he saw firsthand that it didn't have to be that way. That it *wasn't* that way.

That started him thinking.

If being here, working with both teens and horses that the world had all but given up on, could ultimately rescue his soul, maybe it could do the same for other returning soldiers who were trying—and failing—to find a place for themselves in society.

The thought fired him up.

So much so that he decided to bring it to Graham's attention and see what the man thought of it.

And there was no time like the present.

So, hat in hand—literally as well as figuratively—Chance knocked on Graham's door.

"Door's not locked," Graham called out.

Opening the door to the small bedroom that Graham had converted into his office, Chance made no move to enter. "Mind if I talk to you?" he asked, standing just on the other side of the threshold.

Graham beckoned him forward. "Come on in," he invited warmly, turning away from his computer. "What's on your mind? Everything going all right with the boys?"

"Everything's fine," Chance told him. Then he fell silent. The words he had rehearsed in his head on the way over all seemed to disappear. He mentally shook himself, getting back on track. "That's kind of why I'm here."

But he still stood there like a supplicant before his boss's desk, looking no doubt very uncomfortable.

"Why don't you sit down?" Graham suggested, gesturing to the chair before his desk. "Maybe if you take a load off, you'll find it easier to share whatever's on your mind."

Chance took a seat, but he remained ramrod straight. Graham probably thought he looked like an action figure that had been bent into an uncompromising position.

When Chance didn't start talking, Graham's face took on a serious look.

Other than at the dinner table or by the horses, Chance wasn't used to talking to Graham, and he couldn't read the man's expression. He just had a feeling his boss was about to say something bad.

"You're not leaving us, are you?" Graham finally asked him.

It took a second for Chance to replay the question in his mind. "What? Oh, no, no I'm not—unless you're not satisfied with my work," Chance qualified, wondering if perhaps the man was looking for a way to break the news to him.

"Trust me, I am *more* than satisfied with the caliber of your work," Graham told him. "But something must have brought you in here."

Chance cleared his throat. While he was used to going his own way, he wasn't used to being part of a team, and yet that was what he was right now. Part of a team, and making a suggestion that would in turn affect that team.

Chance began to stumble through a response. "Yes, it did."

"I'm listening," Graham encouraged.

In order to make his point, Chance realized that he was going to have to do something he absolutely hated—he was going to have to talk about himself. But there was no way around it because in order to sell his suggestion, he could use only himself as an example.

"When I was first discharged from the military, because of what I had seen, I kind of came apart at the seams and was pretty much at loose ends." Because the story felt too personal to him, Chance kept the details vague and general. "After having seen combat, after watching more than one person's life wiped out in the blink of an eye, nothing seemed all that important anymore. I certainly didn't feel like I fit in to the world I came back to." He moved closer to the edge of his seat, his eyes intently on Graham to see if he was getting his thought across to the man. "There was no place that felt right to me."

"Go on," Graham urged when he paused.

"But when I came here, when I started working with the boys you had on the ranch, with kids who were caught between two worlds, and working with the rescued horses that you stocked the place with, things began to fall into place for me. They started to make sense." His voice took on volume as he warmed to his subject. "I knew why I came back when so many of the other soldiers I shipped out with either didn't come back at all, or came back with their bodies and spirits maimed and damaged. I found my purpose here."

"I'm really glad to hear that," Graham said, and Chance could hear the man's sincerity.

Then Graham leaned forward in his desk chair. Chance had the feeling he knew that Chance wasn't finished, that there was more to the reason why he'd come into his office this afternoon.

Chance ran his tongue along his dried lips, stalling. "So I was thinking…"

Graham was the soul of encouragement. Nodding, he said, "Yes?"

Chance took a deep breath. "I was thinking that if I could feel this way, working with kids who needed help and horses that needed their own form of rehabilitation, maybe in the long run this could work for other soldiers, as well."

Graham kept his gaze even. "Go on."

He'd come this far; he couldn't just let his courage flag now, Chance thought. "What would you think of the idea of opening up a Peter's Place for returning vets?" he asked. Then the next moment, not wanting to put pressure on the man who had given him a second chance to live his life, Chance shrugged evasively and murmured, "It's a dumb idea, huh?"

"No," Graham told him with feeling, "I think it's a great idea."

Chance was as close to being dumbfound as he'd ever been in his life. He felt his excitement growing. "Really?"

"Absolutely." Graham nodded. "In all honesty I always thought that the work we did here could have other uses. Not just for troubled teens. Give me a while to see if I can either find funding for a separate place, or if there's a way to build on to Peter's Place. You know, incorporate the vets and the teens."

This was more than Chance had hoped for. He'd come in expecting Graham to at least listen to his idea, but not to jump on it like this. He was more than delighted.

Apparently so was Graham, as he went on enthusiastically. "The Fortune Foundation's already given us funding to expand the original Peter's Place—that's why you and Chloe are here. Maybe I can talk to the people who hold the foundation's purse strings while they're still feeling generous and see if I can get them to part with a little more money for this added venture. I certainly think it's worth a try—and definitely worthy of consideration."

Graham took a deep breath as he leaned back in his chair. "You have any other suggestions?"

"No, fresh out," Chance told him, spreading his hands out in front of him, a pleased expression on his face. "That was it." So saying, he rose, ready to leave.

"Well, what you came up with was damn good," Graham assured him. "But like I said, let me see what I can do on my end and whose cage I can rattle. And, Chance—?"

Chance stopped on his way out the door, half turned and looked at his boss over his shoulder. "Yes?"

"If you have any other ideas, be sure to come see me with them. I'd be more than happy to hear you out."

Chance grinned broadly, really pleased with how well this had gone. He'd had bosses who had looked upon him as nothing more than a big dumb cowboy. Muscle on horseback. Any minor suggestions he'd tried to make regarding running the ranch had been quickly disregarded. It was nice to be working for someone who regarded him as a person. "Yes, sir, I will. Thank you, sir."

"It's Graham," Graham said, calling after him. "Graham, not 'sir.'"

"Got it," Chance called back, although he had to admit, if only to himself, that it was hard to think of his boss in terms personal enough to refer to him by his first name.

That just wasn't the way he operated.

"Well, you certainly look happy," Chloe observed when Chance walked into the stable a little later that day.

She had arrived a few minutes ago and was saddling her horse. When she hadn't seen Chance here, she'd begun to wonder if maybe he was tired of mentoring her and spending his late afternoon riding with her.

For her, these riding lessons had become the high-light of her day, but she could well understand if Chance was viewing them as time-consuming nuisances.

Then again maybe she was worried about nothing, Chloe thought, because he was here now and he was smiling.

"I am happy," Chance declared, still running on the energy generated by what he felt had been an extremely successful pitch. It amounted to his first small victory in a long, long time.

He was still flying so high on his earlier exchange with Graham that he completely forgot all about being on his good behavior with Chloe—something he'd insti-tuted for himself after that long kiss at the lake. Instead, he took hold of her shoulders and kissed her before he could think to stop himself.

He kissed her hard and with enthusiasm that melted into something more, something meaningful and soul searing. It was only after Chance unlocked his brain and began to think that he realized he'd done it again. He'd gotten carried away.

Chloe made it all too easy to do that.

Releasing her shoulders, Chance still didn't step back immediately. Instead, he forced himself to look into Chloe's eyes, half afraid he would see condemnation there, but nonetheless hoping against hope that what he would find there would be acceptance.

Having been soundly kissed by this handsome cow-boy, Chloe found that, just like the first time, she had to struggle to get air in, struggle not to sound as if she were some addled-brained, incoherent groupie who had just been kissed for the first time.

It took her more than a second to find her mind, which had temporarily gone MIA. When she and her mind were reunited, she was finally able to question him. "Mind if I ask what's made you so happy?"

"I just talked to Graham about the possibility of establishing another center like this one, to help returning veterans. You know, the ones who feel like they're caught between two worlds and don't really belong to either."

It sounded like a noble suggestion to her, and she was proud of him for making it. "What did Graham say?" she wanted to know.

"That he'd look into it." The paltry sentence didn't begin to cover the hope he had attached to the proposed venture.

Chloe felt torn. Torn between being happy for Chance and being unhappy for herself. Because if this suggestion of his worked out and Graham went ahead with establishing a new companion facility to Peter's Place, this one strictly for veterans, she knew that she'd lose Chance. He'd move on, just as she had been afraid he would.

She admonished herself for being selfish. This would help a lot of servicemen if it came to fruition. But she couldn't quite help her emotions.

Feeling almost disloyal, she still had to ask, "Does that mean that you'll be leaving here?"

He honestly hadn't even considered that possibility. He just assumed that if the center he'd suggested turned out to be a separate one, it would still be built some-where within the area. It had to be, he silently insisted.

"What? No," he told her. "I don't want to leave here."

"But if you wind up running this new center for Gra-ham," she began, "wouldn't you have to?"

But there was so much up in the air that Chance didn't want to talk about it right now. And he silenced Chloe the only way he knew how.

By kissing her.

Chapter Thirteen

That kiss by the lake hadn't been a fluke, Chloe realized. It hadn't been just a one-time exhibition of fireworks going off within her and somehow managing to light the darkening skies. Because whatever she'd felt that evening when Chance had kissed her, right now she was feeling that and more.

So much more.

She was feeling almost too much, Chloe realized, a sliver of panic burrowing its way through to her consciousness.

Because of that, *she* was the one who called a halt to the kiss by drawing her head back. Pulling in air, she put her hands up against his chest to serve as a wedge between them.

When Chance looked at her quizzically, undoubtedly wondering why she'd stopped him, Chloe grasped at the first excuse that she could think of.

It was also true.

"Someone might walk in and see us," she warned him breathlessly.

Chance blew out a breath. She was right. What had come over him? They were both in positions of authority when it came to the boys at the ranch. If one of the boys accidentally saw them behaving like hormone-driven teenagers, that wouldn't exactly be the best kind of example for them.

"Right," he murmured, striving to regain control over himself. He flashed her an apologetic look. "Don't know what I was thinking."

Actually, he knew *exactly* what he had been thinking. What he was *still* thinking. That more than anything, he wanted to take Chloe to his bed and make love with her.

But he wasn't about to force his will on her, and if Chloe wasn't interested in making love with him for one reason or another, then that was that.

End of story.

But was it? He couldn't help thinking about that sunset on the lake—and the kiss they'd just shared now. He was certain that he wasn't imagining things. Chloe had kissed him back—with as much feeling as he had experienced himself.

He was just going to have to be patient, he told himself.

"You were probably thinking that we're both human," Chloe said, answering his rhetorical question. "But right now we have to be more than that—for the sake of the boys," she added emphatically. "They look at you as a father figure, you know," she told him.

Since both horses were saddled and ready to ride, Chloe swung onto Mirabel's back and pointed the mare toward the open stable doors.

"Father figure? I wouldn't go that far," Chance told her, easily mounting his stallion and following her out through the doors.

"I would." She knew what it was like to desperately want a father figure in her life and was acquainted with the signs. She saw them in the four teens at Peter's Place, in the way they interacted with Chance. "Because it's true. I think it's a good thing," Chloe went on, seeing she needed to convince him. "All of them need a father figure in their lives. It's an awful thing for a kid when that space is left empty."

He was only vaguely aware of her backstory, her connection to the Fortunes. None of it was his business, he knew that, but he had the feeling that she wanted to talk, so he asked, "You lose your dad early?"

She laughed and he thought the sound was a bit hollow. It made him wonder about what she'd gone through, growing up.

"Yeah, *really* early," she emphasized. "My father was gone before I was born."

"Sorry for your loss," Chance told her, echoing the phrase that people somehow thought was supposed to make up for the pain and cover every sentiment in between mourning and anger. He knew her father wasn't dead, but if he'd been an absentee father, in a way, that was even worse.

Chance sounded genuinely sincere, Chloe thought, and she appreciated it. But the whole tale was just too sordid to get into right now. She was trying to find her purpose here, feeling better about herself because she was reaching out to these boys. For the most part, until just now, she'd managed to focus on the present and not the past.

"It wasn't my loss, it was his." Chloe said. "The man just ran for the hills when he found out my mom was pregnant with me, and he was never heard from again."

She saw that Chance was struggling to find something appropriate to say to her—as if there was such a thing. Which there wasn't.

"It's okay," she assured him. "I got over it. For a while there, I harbored hopes that he'd just come walking back into my life someday, like a scene in one of those 'feel good' movies—you know, the kind that never really happen in real life. But to be honest, I did miss having a father," she admitted. "Until I turned about twelve."

"What happened when you turned twelve?" he asked before he could stop himself.

He realized that perhaps this was going to get way too personal and she was going to tell him about some traumatic event that was better left unsaid. He didn't feel he was equipped to offer her the kind of comfort she might deserve.

She tossed her head almost defiantly, sending her

hair flying over her shoulder. "I decided that it was his loss if he wasn't there, not mine."

There was admiration in Chance's laugh. "You know, you turned out to be a lot feistier than I first thought you were."

"That's what happens when you've got only one parent and you have to half raise yourself," she told him. "Don't get me wrong," she quickly added. "I didn't have the kind of childhood that Will had. I adored my mother and she was my best friend until the day she died. Heaven knew she tried her best to be both mother *and* father to me. But there were times, more than a few," she admitted, "when I was acutely aware that I could have used having a father around, the way a lot of the other girls did."

"So, does it feel any better now?" Chance wanted to know.

"Now?" she questioned, not sure what he was asking her.

He would have thought it was the first thing that came to her mind.

"Well, you're part of the Fortune family now," he reminded her. "That has got to feel different to you, doesn't it?"

"It does," she agreed. "In a way." Chloe searched for the right words to make him understand what was happening and how she felt about it. "But to be honest, I'm not exactly being embraced by one and all and pressed to the bosom of my family."

"Graham hired you." He'd just assumed that was a sign that she'd been accepted.

"Yes," she allowed. "And being a Fortune no doubt had something to do with that. But some of the others— the ones I met at a family dinner at Kate Fortune's last month—they regard me as an outsider, an interloper they made clear they were on their guard against. I got the feeling they thought I wanted more from them than just their acceptance." She was thinking of Sophie Fortune Robinson. The woman had been especially accusatory and downright unkind. Chloe was still trying to get over that ill-fated meeting because it had hurt so much.

And then it dawned on Chloe that she was talking too much, admitting too much. She didn't ordinarily open up like this. Attempting to cover up her feelings, she shrugged.

"That's okay," she said, affecting a careless attitude. "I've been on my own for the most part for so long, I'm pretty used to it. It's nice to have a family, but at this point, if for some reason that changes, I'm okay with that, too."

Chance wasn't buying the nonchalant act. There was a look in her eyes, a distant, wary, hurt look that he didn't know if she was even aware of. But he was. And what it told him was that she had her guard up.

What it didn't tell him was why. He had a feeling that it had something to do with whoever it was whom she had lost—he remembered the one time that she'd let that slip—but until she trusted him enough to really open up, he wouldn't know anything for sure.

"Well, this still looks like a good spot," he said when they came to a stop by the lake—the same exact place he had brought her to that day he'd first kissed her. "Feel like stopping here for a while?"

"Sure, why not?" Chloe thought it looked as perfect now as it had the first time, and it was quickly becoming her favorite place. Dismounting, she saw that Chance had already gotten off his horse and held a blanket in his hands.

"I thought we could just sit here and enjoy the sunset," Chance told her, spreading the blanket on the ground.

"I guess we think alike," she told him. When he stopped to look at her, a question in his eyes, she told him, "I packed a couple of sandwiches for us." She took them out of her saddlebag, along with bottles of water.

They sat down on the blanket. Facing the lake, they watched the sun going progressively lower in the sky as they ate.

When they were finished, Chloe rolled the sandwich wrappers into a transparent ball. "It almost looks like the sun is sinking into the lake, doesn't it?" she observed in hushed awe as she looked on.

"Just gets better every time I see it," Chance admitted.

His words seemed to linger in the air as he turned to look at her.

She told herself that she was imagining things, but it almost sounded as if Chance was applying the words to her as well as to the sunset.

She couldn't help the flash of excitement that went through her veins.

"Does it?" she asked in a hushed whisper.

Chance started to answer.

Or thought he did.

But what he wound up doing was framing Chloe's face with his hands and turning it up to his.

The next moment, he was kissing her again. Kissing her and losing himself in the taste of her mouth, the scent of her breath as she exhaled. Losing himself in the very essence of her.

The sun continued dipping down lower in the sky until it looked as if it was gracefully dancing along the lake's edge, savoring one last moment before it finally vanished completely into the water.

Despite being in the presence of a magnificent display by nature, Chance was aware only of the woman in his arms. How she felt, how soft her lips were, how inviting the press of her body was against his.

And how much he wanted her.

The kisses grew longer.

And deeper.

As did his desire.

His body urged him to go faster, to take what was right there in front of him. But with effort, Chance forced himself to go slow, to not just enjoy her, but to give Chloe the opportunity to consider what was happening between them—and to say no at any point if it came to that for her.

Although he fervently hoped that she wouldn't.

It was inevitable. The more he caressed her, familiarizing himself with every soft, inviting curve of her body, the more he wanted her.

His heart was hammering wildly as he drew Chloe

beneath him on the blanket, slowly exploring every inch of her, finding pleasure in every inch of her and giving her the same pleasure.

And she loved every second of it.

Still, Chloe tried very hard to resist the allure of what Chance promised. Not because she didn't want this to happen, but because she did.

And because she wanted it, guilt hovered on the edges of her consciousness, threatening to break in and shatter everything. That guilt reminded her that she'd already given herself to a man. A man who was no longer able to claim her.

But this feeling that was traveling through her—the desire, the heat, the passion—was exquisite, and she had missed this feeling oh, so much. For the very first time in two years, Chloe felt like she was alive, and she'd missed that feeling.

Missed making love and being made love to.

Her heart was racing like a car at the Indianapolis 500 as her desire for more of Chance's kisses, his touches, just kept increasing at a stunning rate.

She didn't remember tugging off his clothes, didn't remember him pulling hers off, either. But somehow, it had happened because they were on the blanket, naked, their limbs tangled around one another as they lay beneath the full moon, each trying to get their fill of the other.

Each deeply involved in pleasuring the other.

She bit her lip to keep from sighing with delight as she felt his sensual mouth almost artfully glide along her skin, silently claiming everywhere he touched, everywhere he kissed.

Chloe let herself absorb each and every sensation that went spiraling through her body in response to the almost magical things this cowboy was doing to her.

Till her very core felt like an inferno.

She had trouble catching her breath. Her mind scattered in a thousand different directions—which was just as well. She didn't want to think because thinking was bad. Thinking brought guilt, and all she wanted to do was feel. Because in feeling, there was freedom, and what she was feeling had her soaring above the clouds, above everything. As free as a bird.

Finally pulling in a deep breath, she turned and rose above Chance, doing her best to give him back a little of the intense pleasure he was giving her. She'd had only one other partner her whole life, while she was certain that Chance had had many, but she did her best to show him her gratitude for this timeless gift that he was bestowing on her.

After a few moments of reciprocation had passed, he pulled her beneath him again.

He slid his body along hers, sending electric currents of anticipation surging all through her.

Her heart raced faster, all but stealing her breath away.

His eyes met and held hers, communing with her even though not a single word was exchanged. And she answered his unspoken question in kind.

Chance kissed her, then kissed her again. She could feel her body priming.

Waiting.

For him.

When his knee parted her legs, she was ready for him. And then they were joined together, one heart, one mind and one desire overseeing them both.

His body rocked against hers, and then began to move in the timeless rhythm she'd been waiting for.

She moved with Chance, her hips all but sealed to his. The movements grew quicker, stronger as each seemed to anticipate the other, and suddenly they were racing to the end goal, to the explosion that was waiting for both of them.

It seemed to take forever and yet was only as long as a blink of an eye. When it came, rocking them both with its explosion, they clung to one another as if letting go meant extinction.

She could feel her body shuddering, could feel the fireworks receding, ushering in an aftermath awash with a feeling of well-being. She lay there, cradled in the crook of his arm, wondering just how things had come to this moment in time.

She was too tired to come up with an answer, even if it was just for herself.

The sounds of nature were soothing, and she found herself relaxing.

If only for the moment.

Chapter Fourteen

Chloe felt a hand on her shoulder, gently shaking her. Startled, she opened her eyes. Until that moment, she hadn't realized that her eyes had closed or that she'd wound up falling asleep.

"Chloe?" She detected concern in Chance's voice. "Are you all right?"

Embarrassed, flustered, for a second Chloe was at a complete loss for words. They'd made love, and then she'd fallen asleep. What had to be going through his head about her right now?

"I'm okay," she mumbled.

The smile she saw on his lips was totally unexpected. "You're a lot better than 'okay,'" he told her, his smile widening. "But I thought maybe you were upset, you know, now that everything kind of settled down." It was obvious that he must have thought she was only pretending to be asleep.

Chance had never been much for small talk, or really any sort of talk at all. He was a man who believed in doing rather than talking, and as far as he was concerned, his actions—and hers—had done all the talking that was necessary this evening.

But he wasn't so naive or obtuse to believe that men and women thought alike when faced with the same situation. That meant that what was "fine" with him most likely wasn't that way for a woman. Specifically, for Chloe.

So he pressed the matter a little further. "You're not upset or anything, are you?"

"Because we just made love?"

He would have said "had sex," but Chance left it her way and nodded. "Yes."

Chloe took a breath, stalling as she tried to gather her thoughts into a coherent whole. She didn't know what she felt.

Falling asleep beside Chance had to mean that she trusted him, right?

She could see that he was still waiting for an answer. "Well, it wasn't exactly something I'd planned to have happen, especially out in the open like this, but no," she told him honestly after considering the matter, "I'm not upset."

That was a relief, he thought. Out loud, he said, "That's good, because I wouldn't want you to be upset." Replaying his own words in his head, Chance flushed a little. Talking was definitely *not* his strong suit. "Guess that sounds kind of lame to you."

That more than anything else—except for perhaps the way she'd seen him interacting with a couple of the boys—really touched her. Instead of feeling awkward or embarrassed, she felt her heart swelling.

"No," Chloe said, reaching up and lightly caressing his cheek. "As a matter of fact, I think it sounds rather sweet."

"'Sweet,'" Chance repeated, bemused. He laughed shortly. "I don't think anyone's ever called me that before."

"Maybe nobody's ever taken the time to get to know you before," Chloe said. The next second, she realized how that had to sound to him. "Not that I think I know you all that well. I mean—" She was floundering and she knew it. "This isn't coming out right."

Damn, there was just something about her, about the way she talked, even about the way she made mistakes that kept drawing him in.

"I think it came out just fine," he told her right before he kissed her.

He was doing it again, Chloe thought. He was making her head spin. Making her body heat.

It took Chloe several moments before she could finally force herself to draw her mouth back, away from his. It definitely wasn't easy.

"We start doing that again and we're never going to get back to the ranch. Graham's liable to send a search party out for us come morning."

"Wouldn't want to be found like this," Chance agreed. Even to his own ears he didn't exactly sound as if he really meant what he was saying.

She looked beautiful in the moonlight, he thought.

So beautiful that everything he'd felt earlier just before he made love to her was coming back in spades. You'd think that having consumed the forbidden fruit would have negated the overpowering desire for it. But in Chloe's case, it seemed to have just the opposite effect.

Having made love with her had just whetted his appetite for her, because Chance now knew just what was waiting for him.

Rather than let her start getting dressed, the way he knew he should have, Chance lightly brushed his lips against her bare shoulder, sending shock waves through himself—as well as through her.

"One more for the road?" he asked, a very sensual look in his eyes.

The question, so guilelessly asked, had laughter bubbling up in her throat.

"I guess it can't do any harm," she replied, her heart already revving up.

"None whatsoever," he agreed as he pulled her back into his arms.

It began all over again, the thunder and lightning, the excitement, all culminating in a breathtaking shower of stars.

Chloe thought it might prove awkward, running into Chance, having their paths cross half a dozen times a day, not to mention at the dining room table for meals, but it was just the opposite.

It was nice. Very, very nice.

Neither one of them took any liberties with the other or resorted to private jokes or secretive looks that left the others on the ranch guessing. But there was still something enormously comforting about just being around one another.

She wouldn't have given that feeling up for the world.

For one thing, Chloe felt a great deal less alone now. She was still Graham's half sister and Gerald Robinson's offspring, for whatever that was worth, but neither of those two things made her feel as if she was actually part of anything, as if she was connected to anything, despite the implications and despite what Graham had told her when he'd first called her.

But being around Chance and catching glimpses of him during the day *did* make her feel as if she was part of something larger than herself. Something larger and oh, so emotionally comforting.

Chloe knew she was letting herself get carried away and that all this was just temporary, but for now, for this tiny space of time, it didn't matter. She was determined to enjoy this for however long it lasted.

"A family picnic?" Chloe repeated, looking at Graham after he had called her into his small office.

A couple more days had passed and things had been going very well at work as well as during her free hours, but admittedly, in that same time she had barely socialized with her half brother and his family. Despite the fact that they shared some of the same DNA, she still tended to think of Graham more as her boss than as her kin.

And now, out of the blue, Graham had sought her

out to invite her to a family picnic he was planning for that Sunday.

Recalling her last venture into a family function, Chloe had some grave doubts about the invitation. "Are you sure you want me to attend?"

"It *is* a family picnic," he pointed out. "That means it's for both the Fortune family and my work family," Graham explained. "And you actually qualify as both, so yes, I want you to come. Sasha and I both want you to come. Besides," he added, "you're good with Sydney and Maddie."

Now it was starting to make sense to Chloe. "If you need a babysitter—"

Graham was quick to cut her off. "If I wanted a babysitter, I would have said so," he told her. "I was just trying to tell you that the girls would love to see you there, not that we require your services in any other capacity than as an attendee," he said pointedly. Then he added what he felt would cinch the deal for Chloe. "Oh, and Chance should be there."

Chloe looked at him in surprise. "He already agreed to come?"

Graham paused a moment. "He will if he knows that you're going to be there," he admitted. "So what do you say? I'd really like you to come. I'm inviting the boys, too," he added, hoping that would convince her to attend.

Chloe surrendered. She really didn't want to drag her feet about this. "Can't say no to my boss—or to my half brother."

"How about you just call me 'brother'?" Graham suggested. "'Half' brother makes me feel like I've been sliced in two and you get to pick which half you want to deal with. It's not exactly a flattering image," he added.

Chloe grinned. "Well, that's easy enough…"

Graham raised his hand to stop her right there. "I think I'll quit while I'm ahead—provided you did just agree to come to the picnic."

She laughed, knowing that she'd been set up. "How can I say no now?"

"Good, then my plan worked." He picked up the land-line receiver and pulled over a list of phone numbers he'd written down. "Now I have to corral the rest of the people for this picnic."

That caught her by surprise. "I'm the first one you asked?"

"Not exactly," Graham admitted. "I did ask Sasha first. Actually, it was more of a discussion as to what day would be the best to have the picnic. So, in a way, I guess you are the first one." He saw the surprised look on her face. "Why?"

Chloe thought of waving the whole exchange away, but decided, in light of everything, she owed her new-found brother the truth. "I'm used to being the last one asked—to everything—so thank you for that."

"No thanks necessary, Chloe," he responded, already tapping a phone number into the keypad.

Chloe walked out of the office smiling.

When Chance was invited, Graham asked him to extend the invitation to the boys. Like him, they were surprised to be included and at first, all four seemed hesitant to attend what was going to be, after all, a family gathering.

"Why? You need us to act as servers when the food's brought out?" Brandon wanted to know, reverting to his old chip-on-his-shoulder attitude as he posed the question to Chance.

"If you want to help out, that's fine," Chance told the teen, then looked at the other boys who were gathered around him in the stable. "But nobody expects you to. You're just welcome to join in—as guests, just like everyone else."

"Is it mandatory?" Will wanted to know, shifting restlessly from one foot to the other as he eyed Chance.

"It's an invitation, not an order."

"Don't be a jerk," Jonah told the two younger residents. "It's a chance to eat some really good barbecue and be around regular people. Relax. Nobody wants anything from you."

Color crept up Will's shallow cheeks. "I guess you're right," he conceded.

Chance knew the comment from their peer would carry some weight, but he was still grateful when he saw Chloe stepping out of Mirabel's stall, no doubt having heard the entire conversation. He knew she'd add her two cents to the persuasive argument—but only if she felt that he might need backup.

Evidently, she decided he did.

"Old habits are hard to break, aren't they?" Chloe asked knowingly.

The boys turned, almost in unison, to the sound of

her voice. From the looks on their faces, she judged that they hadn't realized that she was anywhere in earshot.

"Sometimes people do things just because they want to be nice without expecting anything in return," she told Brandon and Will. "Get used to it. You'll find that it happens a lot more frequently than you thought—once you put your guard down.

"So," she concluded, looking around at all four of the teens. "Are you guys in?"

Will raised and lowered his thin shoulders in an indifferent shrug. "I guess so."

"Sure," Ryan chimed in with a ready grin.

"I'll be there," Jonah assured them.

"How about you?" Chloe asked Brandon when he kept his silence.

After several beats, Brandon, like Will, shrugged, Unlike Will he avoided looking at either Chloe or Chance when he answered.

"Yeah, I guess so," he mumbled.

"Enthusiasm," Chloe teased, putting her arm around Brandon's shoulders and giving him a quick hug.

Brandon's shoulders were stiff, but she noted with pleasure that he was forcing himself to relax them a little.

Progress!

"I love it," she added.

"Yeah, whatever," Brandon mumbled. For the moment, he let her keep her arm where it was.

"Baby steps, Brandon," Chloe whispered into his ear. "Take baby steps."

"Uh-huh." He shrugged her off, but the moment had

lasted longer than Chloe'd expected. "Well, I got chores to do," he announced to no one in particular.

"Then you'd better get to them," Chance told the boy. He looked at the other three. "How about the rest of you? Stalls cleaned?" he wanted to know.

"Cleaner than our bunks," Ryan volunteered, speaking for the others.

"Then maybe you'd better see about those bunks," Chance suggested pointedly.

The quartet dispersed immediately, one going deeper into the stable, while the other three went to the bunkhouse where they stayed.

"I think that they're coming along pretty well," she said to Chance once the boys were well out of hearing range. She turned toward him for an answer. "What do you think?"

"There's still a lot of work left to do," Chance replied.

He had never been one to allow himself to be overly enthusiastic about something, especially when it was still a work in progress. And that was exactly what he considered the evolution of the four teens to be—a work in progress.

He saw that Chloe was still looking at him, obviously waiting for a positive response.

He sighed, giving in. "But yeah, I think they're coming along. I have to admit that I'm kind of surprised that they're willing to go to this picnic," he told her, lowering his voice in case Brandon could pick up on their conversation.

"Well, I think that it's a hopeful sign," she told him in all sincerity.

He wished he could be as optimistic as she was about this. But life had knocked him around too much. Because of that, he always anticipated the worst.

"Maybe you should keep an eye on them just in case," he suggested.

She wanted to ask in case of what, but there was a bigger question in her mind than that at the moment. "Why? Aren't you going to be there?"

She couldn't think of any other reason for him to say that. Had he changed his mind about going? She was sure that Graham had convinced him to attend. What happened?

"It's a family picnic," he told her, as if that explained everything.

"Not *strictly* family," she reminded him. "Besides, as Graham pointed out, he considers the people at Peter's Place family, too. That means the boys. *And* you," she said pointedly. "Why don't you want to come?"

He frowned slightly, wishing she hadn't put him on the spot like this. "I don't do well in crowd scenes."

That was a lot of nonsense, she thought. "You were in the military. That was a crowd."

"Yeah, and I did my time," Chance pointed out, as if that ended the argument.

Refusing to give up, Chloe tried another tactic. "You can't insult your boss by not showing up. Remember, you're still waiting for his decision on that expansion for a center to help returning vets." She pinned him with a look. "You have to come."

Chance laughed quietly as he shook his head. The woman just didn't give up. There was a time, not all that long ago, when he would have found that to be annoying. But for some reason, not when it came to her.

"You do know how to present a convincing argument," he commented, surrendering.

Chloe's eyes were shining as she replied, "I do whatever I have to do." Then, patting his cheek, she walked out of the stable humming to herself.

Chapter Fifteen

He had told Chloe the truth. He had never really been all that fond of crowds. Wide-open country where a man could travel all day without running into anyone else held far more appeal for him, which was why he preferred spending most of his time on the back of a horse rather than at a table, talking to people he didn't know.

But he had to admit that lately, he had begun to broaden his horizons just a little more. The work he'd been doing with the boys, taking sullen, angry-at-the-world teens who felt that they had been cheated by society and helping them turn their lives around—both by working with them and by his example—had made him reevaluate his take on the world at large.

And then, of course, there was Chloe, Chance thought. He couldn't very well do what he'd done with her on the back of a horse. Not without one of them hurting themselves, he tactfully amended.

Still there was a world of difference between being around Chloe or the boys and these wall-to-wall—or more accurately, he thought, tree-to-tree—people he was looking at today. People who seemed to come in all sizes and shapes, united only by their last name—or at least the DNA that ran in their veins.

Apparently, Gerald Robinson had been extremely generous with his seed, if at times not so generous with his name, Chance thought. The former Jerome Fortune had fathered eight children with his wife, Charlotte. Apparently, that hadn't been enough to satisfy the man. He also snuck around procreating more children—Chloe being one of them—with unsuspecting, easily infatuated young women, leaving them high and dry—and pregnant—as soon as the time seemed right to him.

Chance had to admit that he was surprised to see just how well-adjusted a lot of these people seemed to be, given their background and their father's less than Boy Scout–like history.

But well-adjusted or not, this gathering of Fortune Robinsons and their extended family was just no place for him, Chance decided.

After less than half an hour into it, he began searching for the best time to make his unobserved getaway.

As he moved about, trying his best to look unobtrusive and blend in with the background, Chance suddenly felt someone slip their arm through his. Caught entirely off guard, he turned his head to find that Chloe had quietly walked up behind him.

Chloe returned his rather startled look with a smile. "I know what you're thinking," she told him.

"Oh? And what is it that I'm thinking?" Chance wanted to know, rather impressed by the confidence he heard in her voice.

She knew because in his place, she would have thought the same thing. "You're thinking that it's so crowded here, you could just easily slip away and nobody would notice that you're gone."

She was good, he thought.

"The thought did cross my mind," Chance admitted in a conversational tone.

"Well, they would notice. *I* would notice," she told him, looking at Chance pointedly.

That look in her eyes had him remembering the way she'd been at the lake the other night. And the memories had him fervently wishing they were there alone again right now, instead of milling around in a crowd of people.

"You're just saying that," he told her.

"No, I'm just meaning that," Chloe insisted. "You forget, aside from Graham and Sasha and their kids—" she pointed at the small quartet out in the center of a larger circle of people "—you and the boys are the only other people here I really know."

Something wasn't quite making sense to him. "I thought you said you met these people at a big dinner party at Kate Fortune's ranch last month ago."

"I *saw* them at a big dinner party a couple of months ago," she corrected. "There's a big difference between seeing and knowing. I just recognize some of these people by sight. That's not the same thing," she stressed, wanting him not to feel as if he was the only outsider here.

Still, Chance looked unconvinced by her argument. "Recognizing some of these people by sight is a start," he pointed out.

Chloe laughed as she picked up a paper cup filled with diet soda from one of the smaller tables that had been set up. "Don't try to snow me with rhetoric, Chance. By your own admission, you're not all that good with words."

"No," he agreed, then spared her a meaningful look. A look that instantly made her feel warm and wanted. "I have other talents."

She blushed, unable to stop the surge of color that raced to her cheeks.

"Yes, you do," she quietly admitted. "And I'd really like it if you and your 'talents' stayed awhile longer. And the boys would like it, too."

She pointed them out for his benefit.

He was surprised to see that all four were not that far away from them, caught up in a conversation with one of the other Fortune Robinson family members.

"They're finally beginning to learn how to adapt to people," Chloe told him. "This is very good for them."

He saw her point about how being here was good for the teens, but he didn't see the dots connecting in his case the same way that she did. "Don't see what my leaving or not leaving has to do with them."

Some people needed to be hit by a two-by-four before they understood things, she thought. Chloe tried

her best to get her point across. "Don't you see? You're
their leader. They look to you to set an example. You
leave, it won't be long before they leave."

It was a hell of a burden she was putting on his shoulders, Chance thought. "What about you?"

"I'm not leaving," Chloe answered, deliberately
tightening her arm around his.

"No, I mean, you interact with them. They come to
you for advice on top of those counseling sessions you
have. Why can't *you* be their leader here?" he wanted
to know. That made sense to him.

But Chloe had no intention of giving an inch in this
matter. "Sorry, the role of leader's already been cast,
and it's you," she told Chance, patting his arm with
her free hand. She smiled up into his face. "Deal with
it." Chloe gestured toward the barbecue grills that had
been set up. "Have a burger, have a beer. *Smile.*" The
last seemed almost like an order.

He moved his lips spasmodically in response to the
last word.

Chloe laughed. "That'll do for now."

"Who *are* all these people, anyway?" he asked her,
looking around at the sea of people, both pint-size and
adult.

Chloe looked around, trying to see them through his
eyes. She could understand how all this might be kind
of overwhelming to a loner like him. Being a part of
this family was still overwhelming to her, too.

She took a breath, wanting to get the names and faces
straight in her mind before answering him.

"Well, I don't know all of them," she qualified. "But

over there, next to Graham and Sasha and the girls, are Ben and Ella Fortune Robinson and their newborn, Lacey. Well, she's not a newborn anymore, she's two months old—"

"Practically old enough to go to work," Chance joked.

Relieved that he seemed to be in a better mood, Chloe pointed to another couple.

"That's Ben's brother, Wes, and his new wife, Vivian. Over there—"

She stopped as she suddenly recognized the young woman who had made her feel so unwelcome at the last gathering. For a split second, Chloe thought of turning around and leaving herself—but after what she'd just said to Chance, she knew she couldn't do that. So instead, she mentally regrouped and tried again.

"Over there," she told Chance, "is Sophie Fortune Robinson, and her fiancé, Mason Montgomery."

As covertly as possible, Chloe turned the other way so that Sophie wouldn't see her face if she looked in this direction. All Sophie would see would be the back of her head. One blonde was more or less like any other, Chloe reasoned.

"Now, right over by the lake is Zoe Fortune Robinson. Except she's married now. That's her husband, Joaquin Mendoza, with her."

Because she'd started this, Chloe continued to systematically identify the next cluster of people she recognized even though she suspected that Chance would be perfectly happy if she just stopped right here.

She pointed to the next four people. "That's Olivia

and Kieran, two more of Gerald Robinson's legitimate children. And that guy with the British accent is Keaton Fortune Whitfield. He's one of the…" She hesitated, then added, "…well, illegitimate offspring, like me. And that's his fiancée, Francesca Harriman."

She looked around but didn't find the last Robinson daughter. "Seems the only one missing is Rachel. Graham told me she lives in Horseback Hollow with her husband."

Chance nodded. They were nothing but names to him, but because it meant so much to her, he mentally reviewed the people she'd pointed out. He noticed the expression on the man she called Kieran. "Now, there's a man who looks as unhappy about being here as I am."

Because she'd named so many for him in quick succession, she wasn't sure whom Chance was referring to. "Which one?"

He didn't want to come right out and actually point to the man. That seemed kind of rude. But he had been paying more attention than Chloe probably thought he was.

"That guy you called Kieran," he told her.

She had to admit that Chance had surprised her. She looked over to the man he'd singled out and saw that Chance was right. Kieran did look exceedingly unhappy. Pausing, she recalled what Sasha had told her about his situation.

Things fell into place.

"He's not unhappy because he's here," Chloe told him. "He's worried about Zach."

"Zach," Chance repeated. Another new name. This was getting really complicated. "Maybe I should be taking notes here," he said sarcastically.

She could understand Chance's confusion. There were a lot of names, a lot of details to keep straight. She gave him a quick summary. "Zach is Kieran's best friend, and Zach's been in a coma for a week now, ever since he was thrown by a horse. He suffered a skull fracture. Obviously, not everyone can become one with a horse the way you can," she couldn't help adding.

Chance's immediate response was one of sympathy. "Poor guy." And then he asked, "Is he going to be all right? The guy who got thrown, I mean. Zach," he finally remembered.

"Nobody knows," she told Chance. "But we can ask for an update on his condition."

Taking his hand, she urged Chance to come with her as she drew closer to Kieran.

Chance was reluctant at first. After all, this wasn't any business of his. He didn't know either of the two men involved. But he did know what it was like to be worried about a friend, worried about that friend not making it. That memory would always be very vivid for him, he thought ruefully.

That got the better of him, and he came along with Chloe.

As they drew closer to Kieran, she overheard one of the other people at the gathering asking him about Zach's condition before she had a chance.

"It's the same," Kieran answered. He was toying with the glass of lemonade in his hand, but he had yet to drink any of it. "He hasn't opened his eyes in a week. I've been in the hospital with him every day, and I keep waiting for Zach to sit up and laugh, 'Gotcha!' but he just goes on lying there."

"What about his three-year-old?" someone else spoke up, wanting to know about the man's daughter. "Rosabelle, right? He's the only one she has."

That only added to the sad scenario, Chloe thought.

"Zach's parents have been taking care of her while they've been praying for a miracle. We've all been praying for a miracle," Kieran murmured more to himself than to anyone around him.

"What if there is no miracle?" This question came from Francesca, who looked deeply moved by what she was listening to. "What happens to Rosabelle then?"

Kieran took a deep breath, as if that would give him the strength he was looking for in order to reply. But it wasn't enough. His voice came out quiet, distant. It was obvious that this was not an outcome that he welcomed.

"Then Rosabelle comes and lives with me. Zach asked me to be her guardian." Kieran shook his head. "He must have been out of his mind," he said sadly.

"Or maybe just very intuitive," Chloe told him, speaking up.

Kieran flashed her a grateful, albeit sad smile. "I doubt it," he replied.

"That was a nice thing to say," Chance told her as they moved away from the cluster of people who were around Kieran.

She shrugged off his compliment a bit self-consciously.

"That would be what I'd like someone to say to me under those circumstances," she confided. "Maybe it would even make me feel better."

To Chloe's relief, as the afternoon wore on, Chance no longer looked as if he needed to be tethered in place to keep him from fleeing the premises. And once he relaxed, that in turn had an effect on her, and Chloe felt herself relaxing, as well.

The picnic seemed to go on forever, but it was the good kind of forever, the kind that wound up being one of those memories people looked back on fondly over the passage of years.

Consequently, she and Chance were still at the picnic as the day tiptoed toward twilight.

The conversation, which had revolved around a whole host of different topics, turned to Ariana Lamonte, a reporter, Chloe discovered, who was systematically interviewing various members of the family for a piece the woman was writing entitled "Becoming a Fortune."

From what she was picking up from various family members, it sounded to Chloe like a huge invasion of privacy.

"I don't particularly like her angle on this," Sophie was saying. "She's been doing a lot of hinting that our mother—well, the mother of some of us," Sophie amended, trying to be as tactful as possible given the situation. Taking a breath, the young woman started again. "She's broadly hinting that Charlotte," she said, referring to her mother by her given name, "knew quite a bit more about Dad's cheating on her than she admits to."

"Well, that's because your mother's a smart woman," Sophie's fiancé said. "Let's face it, unless he kept her drugged or locked in a closet, she had to know something."

Chloe caught the indignant look that Sophie shot at Mason, but then she noticed Sophie's face soften. Perhaps because she felt Mason was right, Chloe thought. What Gerald Robinson had done was nothing short of terrible. He had willfully broken his vows and slept with every woman who apparently wasn't smart enough to run for the hills when she met him. Including her own mother.

"Guess we're kind of a sorry bunch," Sophie said to the others.

"Hey, I'm not sorry," Keaton told her. "Because no matter how I got here, I *did* get here," he said with emphasis. "And it doesn't matter who sired you or how. You're here, you're breathing and the rest is up to you from here on in. You've got your own future in your hands," Keaton maintained. "That's not to say that you can't look to family for a little backup," he added with a grin. "And there sure is a lot of family to look to around here."

"I still feel bad about Mother," Sophie told the others.

"Don't," Zoe said. "I'm sure she feels more than compensated for her 'pain and suffering' whenever she takes a look at the bank account balances, or goes shopping in one of those high-end department stores she loves so well."

"That's terrible," Sasha said to Graham, apparently not quietly enough because she was overheard.

"That's life," someone else countered. "Not everyone's a romantic at heart like Sophie."

Appalled at the criticism of a woman she'd never met, Chloe spoke up. "But money doesn't keep you warm at night no matter how much there is of it."

"But it can certainly pay for a really good heating system," one of the other people pointed out, laughing at their own joke.

This was a conversation Chance felt he had no right to be part of, as well as no interest. No doubt it had to be disturbing Chloe, too.

Feeling protective of her, he took Chloe's hand and guided her away.

"C'mon, let's see if we can find something sweet to take the bitter taste out of my mouth," Chance urged, nodding toward some of the tables that were set up beyond the grills. Sasha had several different desserts arranged there, and there were still some left.

Chloe looked around at the picnic gathering. Despite some of the differences of opinion that had been thrown out over the course of the last few hours, she was beginning to believe that maybe, just maybe, she could have it all. A career, a family that numbered more than just one other person and, most important of all, love.

She slanted a look toward Chance, her heart swelling with hope. "Sounds like a good idea to me," she agreed.

Chapter Sixteen

"Chloe, could I speak to you for a minute?"

About to go with Chance to get some dessert, Chloe was stopped dead in her tracks by a familiar voice. The last time she had heard that voice, she was being reviled for having the nerve to crash a family celebration, pretending to be Gerald Robinson's daughter. More things had been said, but Chloe had tuned them out, leaving the party soon after that.

With effort, Chloe forced herself to turn around and face Sophie Fortune Robinson. Although she was doing her best to hide it, an awkward feeling immediately wrapped itself around her. The exact same feeling that she'd experienced at the dinner party when Sophie had cornered her only to give her a complete dressing-down.

Gerald Robinson's youngest legitimate daughter had been furious with her.

Bracing herself for the worst, Chloe said, "All right, I'm listening." *Which was more than you did*, she added silently.

Looking rather uncomfortable herself, Sophie glanced in Chance's direction. "Alone?" she requested.

Chance took his ground. "I can stay with you if you want me to," he told Chloe, deliberately not looking at Sophie. "Or I can wait for you over there." He nodded toward the dessert tables. "Your call."

The fact that he had volunteered to remain with her and was willing to do whatever she wanted heartened Chloe. It also gave her the strength to face whatever it was that Sophie had to say.

Chloe squared her shoulders. "It's okay. Just don't leave," she added as a coda, afraid he might take this opportunity to walk away from the picnic and go back to the bunkhouse.

"I'll be by the dessert table," Chance promised. And then he slanted a glance at Sophie before adding, "Within earshot if you need me."

With that, he walked away.

Stepping over to an area that was temporarily devoid of any picnickers for the moment, Chloe told Sophie, "All right, we're alone—or as alone as we can be at a family picnic." She pressed her lips together, centering herself before asking, "What is it that you want to tell me?"

It took Sophie several moments before she finally said the words Chloe never figured she'd hear.

"I'm sorry."

Chloe didn't know if she was being set up, or if she'd missed something. Sophie had looked almost hostile when their eyes had met that night at the dinner party. She assumed that nothing had changed. Or had it?

"Excuse me?"

"What I said to you the night at Kate Fortune's ranch... Well, I was out of line and I'm sorry. But you have to understand, it was a huge shock to me."

"Finding out that Gerald Robinson was my father?" Chloe asked. "Think how I felt," she pointed out.

Sophie nodded. "All I could think of was how *I* felt. And it wasn't just about finding out about you. It was finding out that the father I grew up adoring was nothing like what I thought he was. That the man I thought was so honorable couldn't seem to remain faithful or true to anyone." Her voice trembled as she spoke. "I was angry, I was hurt and I felt betrayed. And I'm afraid that I took it out on you." She looked at her, clearly embarrassed. "And for that I'm very sorry. I shouldn't have been angry with you. We were both in the same boat."

"Actually, we weren't in the same boat," Chloe politely corrected her. "Yours was a luxury liner. Mine was a leaky rowboat," she said, referring to the fact that while Sophie's childhood was spent in the lap of luxury, hers had been more of a hand-to-mouth existence because her father had deserted her mother.

Sophie's discomfort seemed to increase. "And that makes me feel twice as bad," Sophie told her.

"That wasn't your fault," Chloe pointed out. "That was your father's fault. When my mother finally told me who my father was—that he wasn't her high school sweetheart who was killed in a car accident before he could marry her, which was the story she'd told me all along—she admitted that she'd loved him a great deal. And she told me how devastated she was when he just up and left her."

Chloe felt emotion choke her, and she cleared it from her throat before she continued. "Anyway, that practically destroyed my mother—but she realized that she had to go on living because I needed her, so she pulled herself together and created a life for the two of us.

"Because of the strength she displayed, my mother made me see that we each have the ability to be the masters of our own destinies. That means we can't put the blame on some outside forces that might or might not come swooping in."

As Chloe spoke she saw the shift of emotion on Sophie's face. Her expression went from sorrowful to hesitant and now hopeful. "So does that mean you forgive me?"

"There's nothing to forgive," Chloe told her, wanting to put the matter to rest.

But Sophie wasn't finished atoning for what she'd done. "Still, it took a lot of courage for you to come meet us the way you did, and then having me jump down your throat like that had to have made you feel just awful."

"Well, it didn't make me feel good," Chloe admitted. Since Sophie had apologized, she didn't want the other woman to continue feeling badly. "But if I were in your place, maybe I would have said the same thing."

Sophie shook her head. "No, you wouldn't have—but thank you for saying that," she told Chloe as she hugged her.

A smile bloomed on Chloe's lips. It looked like she was finally being accepted, not just by one or two members, but by the whole family in general.

It felt wonderful, Chloe thought.

Disengaging herself from Sophie, she pointed behind the young woman. "I think someone's waiting for you to get back to him," she told her half sister.

Sophie turned around to see that Mason was standing off to the side, patiently waiting for things to be resolved.

"He's been my rock through this whole thing," she told Chloe. Releasing her, Sophie lingered a moment longer. "We need to get together again—soon," she emphasized sincerely.

"It's a deal," Chloe told her, relieved that Sophie no longer looked upon her as some sort of a troublemaking agitator.

Chloe breathed a sigh of relief as she turned around to look for Chance.

He was waiting for her exactly where he said he would be—at the dessert table.

As she joined him there, Chloe had the impression that he had been watching her the entire time she'd been interacting with Sophie.

When she approached, he said, "I guess you didn't need rescuing after all."

"No, it turns out that I didn't," she told him. "Sophie came to me to apologize."

Ordinarily, he never asked for more information than was offered. But this time, he made an exception. Since he was in the dark about the whole incident at the previous dinner party, Chance asked, "What was she apologizing for?"

Chloe filled him in on the details.

"And she just apologized to you now for having a bad attitude?" he asked.

"I think, in part, she was apologizing for accusing me of lying about the whole thing. I get the impression that until the man's numerous partners came to light, Sophie thought her father walked on water." Chloe shook her head. "I guess it kind of goes along with the way my mother felt about him.

"When she finally told me the truth about who my father was, my mother admitted that she'd literally worshipped him—right up to when he walked out on her and broke her heart." Chloe frowned, thinking back over the years. So much made sense now. "I guess that's why she never got married or even had a relationship. She couldn't bring herself to trust another man enough to let her guard down."

Chance shook his head. He didn't say what he was thinking. That in his opinion, after what Chloe's father had done and all the people he had hurt with his behavior, Chloe's father should have been horsewhipped—at the very least.

"How many illegitimate kids did you say this man has?" Chance asked her.

Chloe sighed. She honestly had no idea how many

there were. It was an odd thing to admit about her own father.

"The final count isn't in yet," she told him when she saw that he was waiting for an answer. "A couple of my half brothers are still trying to track down other potential siblings."

"Damn, that's really one for the books, all right," Chance commented.

It certainly was, Chloe thought, growing quiet. Gerald or Jerome or whatever he chose to call himself now was still her father, but she felt no affection for the man, no desire to be protective of him. She did, however, feel protective of her late mother, and she felt that to criticize the man her mother fell in love with, even temporarily, was to criticize her, and Chloe wouldn't allow that.

When Chance commented on the fact that she had grown very quiet, she deliberately changed the subject by suggesting they find the boys to see how they were faring at the picnic.

It took some looking, but when they did find all four of them, the teens were apparently having a good time, mingling with the younger people who had been brought to the picnic. They were also getting along with one another rather well.

When she saw that, Chloe felt warm all over. She'd been right to talk the boys into coming.

The way she saw it, the picnic, by almost all accounts, was a success.

There was only one downside to the picnic, and it was only a minor by-product, affecting no one but her.

She'd been riding high for almost the entire duration

of the picnic. First because Chance had stayed, as she'd asked him to, and then because he had acted like the perfect hero, offering to stand by her. But now Chloe began to examine her feelings for Chance as well as what she'd hoped was her developing relationship with him.

The conclusion she came to was that any way she looked at it, Chance was too good to be true.

The phrase stunned her, echoing in her brain.

She realized that these were the exact same words her mother had used to describe the man who was her father. The man who had ultimately just run out on her, disappointing her so badly that he had crushed her young heart and prevented her from ever venturing to love anyone again.

That had to have been so emotionally crushing for her mother, Chloe thought. Even so, her mother had refused to crumble. Instead, she became a strong woman who had gone on to make a life for the two of them.

Admittedly, Chloe didn't know what she would have done if she'd been in her mother's place. What she did know was that she never *wanted* to be in her mother's place.

Too good to be true.

The phrase continued to echo in her head each time she looked at Chance. How could she expect a man like him to remain with her? To love her?

She knew the inevitable answer to that.

There was something she needed to do, Chloe decided, if she didn't want to be hurt the way her mother had been. She needed to make a preemptive strike in order to save herself.

* * *

The thought haunted her for the next few days, growing progressively larger and larger in her mind until it felt as if there was nothing else on her mind except for that.

"Miss Elliott? Are you okay?"

Chloe realized that she'd allowed her thoughts to get the better of her—again. It had been happening to her for days. In this case, instead of listening to Will and responding, she'd drifted off.

She looked at the boy apologetically. She couldn't afford to jeopardize the progress he and the others had made by allowing herself to become obsessed with her personal life. That wasn't fair to the boys, and it just wasn't right.

"I'm sorry, Will. I'm afraid I was just thinking about something."

"Yeah, I can tell." A shy smile curved the boy's mouth. "I asked you a question three times and you didn't answer."

Chloe looked at him, appalled. "Three times? That's unforgivable," she told the teen.

"Well, maybe it was two," he admitted, shrugging his thin shoulders. "But you did look like you were really far away. Anything I can help with?"

How far the teen had come, she thought. She was proud of having had a hand in his progress. She didn't want to be the cause of its undoing. "No, but you're a doll for asking."

Will flushed. "You're not going to call me that in

front of the other guys, are you?" he asked, clearly hor-
rified at the possibility.

She struggled not to laugh at the look on his face.
"Your secret's safe with me, Will," she assured him,
then, in case there was a question, she added, "*All* of
your secrets are safe with me. You know that."

Will nodded. Their session was over and he had
homework waiting for him, so he needed to go.

"Yeah, that's what you said when we started these
things," he said, referring to the sessions as he got up.
And then he stopped to look at her. "Um, Miss Elliott,
you know that goes both ways, right?"

"I'm not sure I understand, Will," Chloe admitted.

Rather than just retreat, the way he would have a few
short weeks ago, Will tried to explain. "What I'm trying to say is that if you've got something you want to
talk about to someone, you can talk to me. I'm a good
listener," he told her. "And I won't tell anyone anything. I promise."

She was tempted to hug him, but she knew how frag-
ile teen egos were. She didn't want him thinking she
regarded him as a child. He was a budding adult. So
she kept her arms at her sides and simply told him, "I
appreciate that, Will."

Even so, she wasn't about to tell him or any of the
boys what was on her mind, especially since it involved
Chance.

"But there's nothing I need to talk about," Chloe said.

There was something, though, she thought, that she
needed to *do*. And soon.

But it wasn't going to be easy.

* * *

She'd agonized over it the entire day, until it was finally time for what had become a minor ritual: going out riding with Chance at the end of the day. She knew she couldn't put this off any longer. Because the longer she did, the harder it was going to be for her.

When Chance walked into the stable, expecting to go riding with Chloe as he did every late afternoon, he was surprised to see that although she was there, her horse wasn't saddled yet.

"You just get here?" he wanted to know. Even that was unusual for her. Punctuality was a thing for Chloe. She didn't like being late.

As he looked at her, he sensed the tension in the air and couldn't help wondering what was wrong. Rather than push, he waited for her to answer.

"Actually, I've been here for a while, waiting for you." Every word felt as if she was dragging it out of her mouth from the very depths of her soul. And every word tasted bitter on her tongue.

Her answer didn't make any sense to him. He frowned. "But your horse isn't saddled. Something wrong?" he asked, subconsciously trying to brace himself.

She didn't answer his question directly. Instead, Chloe went on to say the hardest words that she had ever had to say. "I don't think that we should go out riding together anymore."

"Okay." He regarded her warily as he spoke. Still, he had to go on as if everything was all right. Because he really wanted it to be. "You want to do something else instead?" Almost every time they went out, they returned to end their day in the guesthouse, enjoying each other's company to the fullest.

He had a feeling that wasn't going to be the case today, but he still had to ask.

She shook her head. "No, you don't understand. I don't think we should do anything together—including what we do after we go riding," she added, deliberately being vague because she didn't think she could say anything more specific without breaking down. As it was, she was fighting back tears. Her throat felt as if it was closing up.

She was looking away. Gently taking her face between his hands, Chance forced her to look up at him. "Have I done something to offend you?"

"No, you've been perfect," she cried, pulling back. Needing to put distance between them. "You've always been perfect."

It almost sounded like an accusation, he thought. One that just didn't make any sense at all. "I don't understand."

Tears were welling up in her eyes, and she looked away, not wanting him to see her cry.

"Please, don't make this any harder than it already is. I just can't see you anymore."

"Did Graham say something?" he asked, trying to make sense out of what was happening. Was there some sort of nonfraternizing rule in place that he didn't know about? If there was, then he'd quit. She meant that much to him.

For the first time in years, he'd been able to get beyond himself, and it was all because of her. And now she was pulling back. It didn't make sense to him, and he needed to know why this was happening.

"No, nobody said anything, and it's not anything you did." Her voice cracked and she tried again. "Please, Chance, don't ask me any more questions."

He felt as if he had been sliced in half, and he had no idea why or even what had gone wrong. All he knew was that he needed to get out of there now, while he could still function.

Before he couldn't move.

"All right," he told her stiffly, "I won't."

It was the last thing he said to her before he walked out.

His voice echoed in the stable long after he left. Just as long as she went on crying.

Chapter Seventeen

It's better this way. It's better this way, you know that. Better to stop this now, before you give away your heart. You know what happens after that.

Chloe kept telling herself that over and over again, and while she believed she had done the right thing, that still didn't make it any easier for her to live with. She tried to keep as busy as possible, but a sadness saturated her every waking moment.

Especially the evenings, which now seemed to last twice as long as they used to.

But the hardest part was running into Chance. Their paths seemed to cross a lot less than they used to, but when they did, she felt an unbearable pain, as if she'd been stabbed by a sword with rusty, jagged edges every time she realized that he was there, somewhere near her space.

When was it going to get better? When was the pain going to go away? She had broken things off with Chance to avoid being hurt and yet, that was exactly what was happening. Pain, raw and devastating, was eating her up from the inside out.

In its own way, this was every bit as difficult to endure as when she'd found that Donnie was no longer going to be part of her life, that he'd never be coming back to her.

Chloe began to second-guess herself. Had she acted too rashly? In trying to avoid heartache, had she unwittingly opened the door and allowed heartache to come into her life?

Chloe had no answers, only more questions.

"How come you don't go riding with Ms. Elliott anymore?" Brandon asked out of the blue one afternoon as he and Chance were in the corral, working on taming a new addition to the herd that Graham had just bought.

Chance had picked Brandon to help him because the teen showed the most promise when it came to working with the horses. His hostility finally under control, Brandon was usually on the quiet side. But that obviously wasn't the case today.

"That's not a question you should be asking me," Chance told him.

"I thought you told me that I could ask you anything," Brandon said innocently.

The horse was fighting the bit he was trying to put

into its mouth. For the moment, Chance stopped to look at Brandon. "About your own life, not mine."

"Well, since I've been here, you've become part of my life," Brandon pointed out. "You and Miss Elliott." Determined to get an answer, he tried again. "So how come you don't go riding together anymore?"

"It's just better this way," Chance told the teen dismissively, hoping that would be the end of it.

It wasn't.

"Doesn't seem better," Brandon observed after several minutes. He stroked the stallion's muzzle, doing what he could to keep the animal calm as Chance made another attempt to put the bit into the stallion's mouth. "Seems like both of you look real unhappy. If things were better, you two wouldn't look like that."

Chance sighed. *No arguing with that*, he thought. "It's complicated."

"That's what people say when they don't want to talk about something—or admit that they're wrong about something," Brandon added. "From where I'm sitting," he continued when Chance made no comment, "it doesn't look complicated at all. You were happy riding together, and now you're not riding together and you're not happy. Seems to me like you were both better off riding."

The third attempt to get the horse to accept the bit succeeded. Chance paused, not wanting to rush things with the stallion.

"Yeah, well, that's not going to happen," he told Brandon as he fed the horse a lump of sugar. "Get the blanket."

Brandon did as he was told, hurrying to the fence where the blanket hung and then back again. He held it out to Chance, along with more advice. "You could tell her you're sorry."

Chance handed the reins to the teen and spread the blanket on the horse's back. The stallion remained relatively still. "What?"

There was a warning note in Chance's voice, but Brandon pushed on anyway.

"If you made her angry," Brandon explained, "you could tell her you're sorry. Women like it when you tell them you're sorry."

The assertion by one so young made Chance laugh. "And how would you know that?"

"That's what my brother told me," Brandon said matter-of-factly. "You know what else he told me?"

Chance paused. He realized that this was a breakthrough for Brandon. Up until now, the teen hadn't talked about the brother he'd lost. He'd acted on the anger he felt because of the loss, but he had never mentioned Blake in a day-to-day context, never even referred to him.

There was a momentary tug-of-war within him, and then Chance decided to set aside his need for privacy, putting Brandon's need to heal and progress ahead of his own. "No, what else did he tell you?"

A distant, wistful look came over the teen's face as he no doubt thought of his brother. "That if you want something, sometimes you've got to fight for it. That if something just falls into your lap, it doesn't mean nearly as much as it does if you have to go out and fight for it."

Brandon grew very solemn as he recalled his brother's words. "That's what Blake told me when I asked him why he enlisted instead of going to college like he was supposed to. He said he had to fight for what he believed in. Maybe that's what you need to do," Brandon concluded, looking at him. "Maybe you need to fight for Miss Elliott."

Chance shook his head. "I don't think Miss Elliott wants me to fight for—"

"I think she's looking pretty sad lately," Brandon stressed. "And Will said she keeps losing her train of thought during his sessions. Ryan says the same thing," he added. "Maybe like she's always saying, you need to talk about it. About whatever it is that made the two of you stop doing what you both liked doing." The teen gave Chance an encouraging smile. "Might make you both feel better about things if you clear the air."

Chance looked at the boy he had been trying to reach for weeks now. The boy who had just now tried to reach him instead.

"It just might at that," he agreed. "But right now, we've got a horse to work with."

"I don't think he'd mind waiting," Brandon speculated.

"Get the saddle." He indicated where he'd placed it on the top rung of the corral. "Always finish a job you start."

"That's a good one," Brandon said, nodding with approval as he went to fetch the saddle. "You might want to remember that one when you go talk to Miss Elliott later," he suggested.

Chance grinned as he took the saddle from Brandon and placed it carefully on the stallion's back. The horse tried to pull away, but Brandon was holding firmly on to the bit, keeping the animal in place. Chance slowly tightened the cinch, watching the horse intently.

"I might at that," Chance agreed.

For the first time since he'd arrived at Peter's Place, he saw Brandon grin.

"Come in," Chloe said in response to the knock on the door of her small office.

When she looked up from her work, she was surprised. Expecting to see one of the boys coming in for what she assumed was an extra session, she found herself looking up at Chance instead.

Her heart leaped, and she felt the definite rush of adrenaline surge through her veins before she managed to tuck it away and get it under control. She wasn't supposed to be reacting to Chance like this anymore, she upbraided herself. Especially since in the days that followed her breaking it off with him, Chance hadn't attempted to approach her, not even once. That convinced her that her so-called preemptive strike in pushing Chance out of her life before he walked out on her had been the right move. Because if he'd actually cared about her—even a little—he would have at least *tried* to get back into her life, tried to get her to give him a second chance.

But he hadn't.

Instead, he'd kept his distance. Even at the table,

when they took their meals, he didn't say even two words to her. A man who cared didn't behave that way.

A man who was glad things were over, however, did.

Not waiting for Chance to say anything that she might not want to hear, she took the lead. Doing her best to sound cheerful, she said, "I hear congratulations are in order."

For a moment, because he was still trying to sort his thoughts out and find the right words to say to her, Chance didn't know what she was referring to. He looked at her, puzzled. "For what?"

"For getting Graham to approve your idea. He seemed very enthusiastic about it," she added, recalling the look on her brother's face when he told her the news.

Because of what he'd been going through, Chance had almost forgotten that his proposal had been approved. Graham had gotten the funding, and plans were under way for expanding Peter's Place to include a military equine therapy center for returning vets. "Oh. Right. Thanks."

She would have thought that he would be happy about his victory. Why wasn't he? "Well, you don't sound like you're nearly as excited about it as Graham is," Chloe observed.

"Right now, that's not the main thing on my mind," Chance admitted, his eyes meeting hers.

She wished he wouldn't look at her like that. It made her remember. And yearn. She had to keep herself from squirming.

"Is there something I can help you with?" Chloe asked stiffly.

She sounded like a robot, Chance thought. Was it because he was here? He began having second thoughts about the whole thing. Maybe this wasn't such a good idea.

But he *was* here now, so he might as well say what he'd come to say. He knew Brandon would ask him about it. Just as he knew that he had to give this one final try so that he knew he had done all he could before giving up on the situation.

On her.

On them.

Here goes nothing. "You can help me understand why you suddenly decided to pull back. I thought things were going pretty well," he told her, forcing himself to be honest about his feelings. "I realize that I don't measure up to your late husband, but—"

She stared at him, stunned. "Wait, what? Who told you about Donnie?" she wanted to know. She had never said anything about her late husband to Chance, never mentioned how distraught she'd felt about losing him. How had he found out?

Chance didn't see how that was the point, but he answered her question. "Sasha told me. Don't blame her, I made her tell me. I asked if you were involved with anyone. I thought maybe that was why you didn't want to go riding with me anymore. Or anything else for that matter," he added meaningfully.

He'd missed being with her more than he could possibly say, but it was hard for him to actually admit that. "She told me that you were devastated by your husband's death."

He'd done his homework, contacted people he knew, people he hadn't spoken to in years and asked questions about the man.

"I know I don't measure up to him in your eyes, but I don't want to take his place. I just want to be with you." She was seated at her desk, and he stood over her now, looking down into her face as he searched for an answer. "Why can't I be with you?"

"Because you're perfect," she blurted out, "and before long, you'll realize that you can do a lot better than me and you'll move on. I just can't take dealing with loss again," she informed him, sadly adding, "This way is better."

His thoughts had come to a grinding halt several sentences ago. "Hold it. You think I'm *perfect*?" he questioned incredulously. "You're pulling my leg, right? I mean, you can't be serious." He was as far from perfect as a man could be, Chance thought.

"Of course I'm serious," she told him. "Why wouldn't I be?"

"Well, for one thing, because I'm not perfect," he told her with a disparaging laugh. Thinking back on the image he'd portrayed to her, he realized how he might have misled her. "I just wanted you to see the best in me because a really classy lady like you isn't going to want to be with any ol' cowboy, especially one that's got his own set of demons."

Despite everything, she couldn't help the smile that rose to her lips. Couldn't keep it from curving the corners of her mouth.

"Haven't you heard?" she asked him. "That's what

I do. I exorcise demons." Her smile faded a little as she grew more serious. "But you never indicated that you were anything but a tall, silent cowboy, the kind that used to be in all those old Westerns that they made in the fifties and sixties."

"A cowboy, yeah," he scoffed. "A cowboy who fought overseas."

Why would he think that changed anything in the way she saw him? "At least you got to come back."

He didn't see that as a plus. It was more like his cross to bear. "At times, I really feel that I shouldn't have."

That made absolutely no sense to her. "Why?" she cried.

He told her what weighed most heavily on his conscience, something he hadn't shared with anyone since he'd returned stateside.

"Because I couldn't save my best friend," he confessed. "Evan and I had been friends since grammar school. We enlisted together, did everything together." His mouth felt dry as he relived his friend's final moments. "Evan got between me and enemy fire. He died in my place, in my arms. And I haven't been able to find a place for myself since." Chance took a breath, and then he looked down at her. She had made the difference in his life. "Until I met you."

"But when I said that we shouldn't be together, you just accepted it," she pointed out. "If I meant that much to you, why did you just back off and not even *try* to get me to change my mind?"

He wasn't the type to push himself on anyone. "Because that's what I thought you wanted, and I wanted you to be happy even if I wasn't."

That sounded like him, she realized. "What changed your mind?"

He laughed softly to himself before answering. "Brandon."

"Brandon?" she repeated. Brandon hardly talked now that he had stopped being angry at the world. "What could he have possibly said to change your mind?"

"He noticed how unhappy I looked. How unhappy we both looked," Chance emphasized. "Then he told me something his brother told him."

"His brother? He opened up about Blake?" Chloe asked, stunned and excited at this breakthrough. Brandon had been her last holdout.

"Yes, he did. He told me that his brother told him very simply that if he wanted something, really wanted it, he should go for it. Fight for it." Chance paused, looking at her pointedly. "So this is me, 'fighting for it.'" He took her hands in his and brought her up to her feet. "Fighting for you." He drew her into his arms and bent his head, kissing her.

Chance's kiss felt as if the sun had suddenly come out after days of being hidden behind a dreary rain cloud. This was what she'd missed, what she'd longed for.

What she'd *needed*.

She kissed Chance with all the bottled-up passion she'd been trying to convince herself she no longer felt. Wrapping her arms around his neck, she clung to him for a moment, her lips sealed to his.

When he finally drew back, he smiled into her eyes.

"Does this mean you'll go riding with me again?" he asked. There was a trace of mischief in his eyes.

"It does," she told him.

Maybe he was pushing his luck, but he still wanted to ask. "Does this also mean that you'll—"

Her eyes danced as she cried, "Yes."

He laughed. She was getting ahead of herself. "I haven't finished asking you the question."

The smile that lit up her features was warm, sunny. And oh, so relieved. "I have an idea I know what's coming."

"I have an idea that you don't," he told her. He knew he had to get this out before his courage deserted him, and he really wished he had something to give her to seal this moment. "Chloe Elliott, I don't have much to offer you—"

How could he even think that? "You're wrong," she told him. "You have a great deal to offer."

"Don't interrupt," he said. "I have to get this out before I lose my nerve."

"All right," she told him, her heart pounding madly. It wasn't easy for her to keep quiet, but she did her best. "Go on."

He started again. "I don't have much to offer you, but I love you and I'll do everything in my power to make you happy—and to never regret marrying me." He stumbled a little, his thoughts getting in the way of his tongue. "That is, if you *want* to marry me." He blew out a breath. "This isn't coming out the way I want it to. Talking isn't what I do best."

She was nothing if not encouraging. "You're doing great so far."

He took a long breath. If he talked any more, he'd mess it up. "I'm finished," he told her. "You can answer now if you'd like."

"I like," Chloe told him with all sincerity. "I like very much."

Maybe this wasn't a total disaster after all. "So will you marry me?" he wanted to know.

Her eyes crinkled as she laughed. "What do you think?"

She was drawing this out, and he couldn't stand the tension pulsating through him. "I think I'm going to have heart failure if you don't answer me in the next couple of seconds."

She kept as straight a face as she could. "I don't know CPR, so I guess I'd better say yes." And then every single part of her being grinned. "Yes, I'll marry you. Yes, yes, yes," she cried, throwing her arms around his neck again.

"I heard you the first time," he answered, gathering her in his arms.

"I wanted to be sure you did."

"I did," he answered, then added, "I do," before he kissed her again.

And, just to be sure that she wasn't going to change her mind, he went on kissing her for a long time.

Epilogue

"So, how did it feel to find out that your father is one of the famous Fortunes?"

The question came from Ariana Lamonte, the magazine writer and blogger who had already interviewed several of Gerald Robinson's children.

They were sitting in the living room of the guesthouse where Chloe was presently living, and the vivacious reporter had already asked her a number of probing questions.

At first, Chloe had thought she was just going to avoid the woman, but after the reporter had called her a number of times in the last few days, Ariana didn't give her the impression that she was about to give up until she got what she wanted. And besides, submitting to the interview seemed almost like an initiation into the family. Others had done it, and if her responses and feelings were put down on record, then by all rights that made her a part of the family, as well.

"It felt strange," Chloe admitted, answering Ariana's last question.

The woman's fingers flew over her small laptop, making notes as thoughts occurred to her.

She looked up at Chloe, giving her a sympathetic smile. "That's right, he was AWOL for most of your life, wasn't he?"

"Not most," Chloe corrected. *"All."*

Ariana nodded, her keyboard clicking rhythmically as she made more notes. "So what did you think of him when you two finally met?"

"We haven't." When Ariana looked at her sharply, she added, "Yet."

"But you're going to, right?" the woman with the long brown hair and the animated, deep brown eyes pressed. "Now that you know who he is, you can't just *not* meet the man," Ariana insisted.

"There's been talk about setting something up, yes," Chloe replied vaguely.

And there was. Gerald Robinson had actually reached out to her. But, still harboring anger over the way the man had treated her mother, Chloe was in no hurry to meet her father face-to-face. She had stalled.

"Aren't you at least curious what he's like?" Ariana wanted to know.

She supposed she was somewhat curious. She wouldn't be human if she wasn't. "Maybe a little," she admitted.

Ariana laughed. She paused and reached over to

lightly touch Chloe's hand. "Well, if it were me and my absentee daddy had all that money—"

"I don't care about the money," Chloe told her, cutting the woman off.

Ariana could only shake her head. "Well, you're a better person than most," she confided.

Chloe set her jaw. "There are some things that money can't pay for. But I will give him a chance to explain why he did what he did—if he actually has a reason."

Ariana smiled warmly at the young woman sitting across from her. "You're a good person, Chloe Elliott. Or would you rather I called you Chloe Fortune? Some of your siblings have taken on the name," the reporter said.

"I'd rather you just called me Chloe," she told the reporter.

"I think I'd like that," Ariana replied. She closed her laptop. "Well, I think I have everything I need," she said, concluding the interview as she rose to her feet. "If I think of any further questions, I'll give you a call. And after you meet your father face-to-face, I'd appreciate it if you give *me* a call," she requested.

Chloe accompanied her to the door.

"Thanks for your time," Ariana told her. "I'll email you a copy of the interview when it's finished."

As she began to walk out, the woman nearly collided with Chance, who was just about to knock on Chloe's door.

"I can see why you were in a hurry to wrap this interview up," Ariana said, looking appreciatively at the tall cowboy, then gave Chloe a grin. "Maybe I'll see you again."

The moment the reporter crossed the threshold and left the house, Chance closed the door behind her. He flipped the lock in place.

"So, how was it?" he asked Chloe, turning to face her.

"Not as bad as I thought," Chloe confessed. "She was nice. She asked a lot of questions, but I think that I managed to hold my own."

"I knew you would," Chance told her. He pressed a kiss to her temple as he gave Chloe a quick, warm embrace.

"Well, that puts you one up on me." She looked away from the door and turned her face up to Chance. She knew he had just come from a meeting with Graham about the planned expansion. "So, tell me," she urged, waiting for him to share his news.

"Everything's in motion," he told her happily. "With any luck, the military *equine*—" he deliberately drew the word out to emphasize it "—therapy center will be opening ahead of schedule. I can't tell you how good that makes me feel."

"Oh, I think I can guess," she told him, amusement dancing in her eyes.

He knew he needed to put this in perspective for her. He wanted her to understand just what she meant to him. "Almost as good as knowing that you're actually going to be marrying me. You still are, aren't you?" he asked, closing his arms around her.

Chloe's smile was wide and warm. "Try to stop me," she told him with a laugh.

"Now, why would I want to do that?" he questioned as if she had just suggested something completely absurd. "My mamma didn't raise any stupid children."

"Good. Neither did mine. Wanna go for a ride?" she asked him.

"Why don't we skip going for a ride today?" he suggested. "And just go straight to the good part."

"I thought you once told me that riding was the good part," she reminded him.

"I did and it was—until I met you and found a whole other way to feel good." He pulled her tighter. "No more talking," he said as he lowered his mouth to hers.

One touch of his lips had desire streaking through her. "No more talking," she agreed.

So they didn't.

* * * * *

COMING NEXT MONTH FROM

H HARLEQUIN

SPECIAL EDITION

Available March 21, 2017

#2539 FINDING OUR FOREVER
Silver Springs • by Brenda Novak
When Cora Kelly gets a job at the boys' ranch run by her birth mother, Aiyana Turner, she thinks she has a year to get to know her mother without revealing her identity. But she never thought she'd fall in love with Aiyana's adopted son, Eli. Once that happens, she's forced to broaden the lie—or risk telling a very unwelcome truth.

#2540 FROM FORTUNE TO FAMILY MAN
The Fortunes of Texas: The Secret Fortunes • by Judy Duarte
Kieran Fortune becomes an instant father to a three-year-old when his best friend dies in a ranch accident. Dana Trevino, his friend's ex-girlfriend, steps in to help the floundering single dad, only to find herself falling for a man she considers way out of her league!

#2541 MEANT TO BE MINE
Matchmaking Mamas • by Marie Ferrarella
First they were playground pals and then college rivals. Now Tiffany Lee and Eddie Montoya are both teachers at Los Naranjos Elementary School, and it looks like the old rivalry may be heating up to be something more when their classrooms go head-to-head in the annual school charity run.

#2542 MARRIED TO THE MOM-TO-BE
The Cedar River Cowboys • by Helen Lacey
Kayla Rickard knew falling in love with Liam O'Sullivan broke the rules of the bitter feud between their families, and she thought she could keep their impromptu marriage a secret. That was, until her pregnancy changed everything!

#2543 THE GROOM'S LITTLE GIRLS
Proposals in Paradise • by Katie Meyer
Dani Post was on the fast track to success before tragedy left her craving the security and routine of home. But when she falls for a handsome widower and his twin girls, she realizes she must face her past if she's going to have any chance of making them her future.

#2544 THE PRINCESS PROBLEM
Drake Diamonds • by Teri Wilson
Handsome diamond heir Dalton Drake struck a royal bargain to give shelter to Aurélie Marchand, a runaway princess in New York City, but falling in love was never part of the deal!

YOU CAN FIND MORE INFORMATION ON UPCOMING HARLEQUIN® TITLES, FREE EXCERPTS AND MORE AT WWW.HARLEQUIN.COM.

HSECNM03

Ben handed Laney a sealed envelope, then walked around the back of the partial chair. "Quite a project you've got here."

"I probably should have taken a nap after the first one." She peeled the flap off the envelope and pulled out a folded paper.

Inside was a short, handwritten note. *I think you should go for it.*

All of a sudden, her cheeks felt warm and she wanted to hide the words against her chest or crumple the paper so there was no chance Ben could read it, even though he'd probably have no idea what her cousin meant by it. Instead she refolded the paper and slid it back into the envelope. Then she pressed the flap down the best she could before lifting the toolbox and sliding it underneath.

"Everything okay?" he asked.

"Yeah." She looked up at him, her mind flailing for some reasonable explanation why Nola would ask Ben to deliver something to her. "Just some information I needed about getting a Maine driver's license and plates for my car and... stuff."

Please don't ask me why she didn't just call or text the information, she thought as soon as the words left her mouth.

"Cool. Do you need some help with this chair?"

"No, thank you. I've got it."

"Want some company?"

"Sure." She wondered if he'd make it five minutes before he leaned in and tried to tighten a bolt for her before just building the rest of it himself. "Want a drink?"

He held up an insulated tumbler as he sat in her folding camp chair, shaking it so the ice rattled. "I have one, thanks. Do you need a fresh one?"

Laney kept her face down, looking at the instruction sheet, so he wouldn't see her smile. He was so polite, but she didn't want to imagine him in her camper. He wasn't as tall as Josh, but he had broad shoulders and she could picture him filling the space. If they were both in there, they'd brush against each other trying to get by…and her imagination needed to change the subject before she started blushing again.

"No, thanks," she said. "I'm good."

"Okay. Yesterday's accident aside, how are you liking the Northern Star? And Whitford in general, I guess."

"I haven't seen too much of Whitford yet. The market and gas station, and the hardware store. And obviously I'll be going to the town hall soon."

"You haven't eaten at the Trailside Diner yet?"

"No, but Nola brought me a sandwich from there yesterday. Right before the accident. It was really good."

"Their dinner menu is even better."

Was he working his way around to asking her out to dinner? It had been so long since she'd dated, she wasn't sure if she was reading too much into a friendly conversation. But it seemed her next line would naturally be *I'll have to try it sometime* and then he'd say *How about tomorrow night?* or something like that.

And she had no idea how she felt about that.

Don't miss
WHAT IT TAKES:
A KOWALSKI REUNION NOVEL
by Shannon Stacey, available wherever books are sold.

www.CarinaPress.com

EXP0317WITSS

JUST CAN'T GET ENOUGH?

Join our social communities
and talk to us online.

You will have access to the latest
news on upcoming titles and special
promotions, but most importantly,
you can talk to other fans about your
favorite Harlequin reads.

Harlequin.com/Community

Facebook.com/HarlequinBooks

Twitter.com/HarlequinBooks

Pinterest.com/HarlequinBooks

Turn your love of reading into rewards you'll love with

Harlequin My Rewards

**Join for FREE today at
www.HarlequinMyRewards.com**

Earn **FREE BOOKS** of your choice.

Experience **EXCLUSIVE OFFERS** and contests.

Enjoy **BOOK RECOMMENDATIONS**
selected just for you.

PLUS! Sign up now
and get **500** points
right away!

Earn
FREE
REWARDS
HarlequinMyRewards.com
Join
Today!

MYR16R

THE WORLD IS BETTER WITH

Romance

Harlequin has everything from contemporary, passionate and heartwarming to suspenseful and inspirational stories.

Whatever your mood, we have a romance just for you!

Connect with us to find your next great read, special offers and more.

f /HarlequinBooks

🐦 @HarlequinBooks

www.HarlequinBlog.com

www.Harlequin.com/Newsletters

HARLEQUIN®

A *Romance* FOR EVERY MOOD™

www.Harlequin.com